Thank you so much for your support,

Best,

John

Thank you so much
for your support Dr. Tuli.

Rafiq

Adventures in the Fantastic

J.M. McKeel

Copyright © 2016 John Michael McKeel.

All rights reserved. No part of this book may be reproduced, stored, or transmitted by any means—whether auditory, graphic, mechanical, or electronic—without written permission of both publisher and author, except in the case of brief excerpts used in critical articles and reviews. Unauthorized reproduction of any part of this work is illegal and is punishable by law.

This is a work of fiction. All of the characters, names, incidents, organizations, and dialogue in this novel are either the products of the author's imagination or are used fictitiously.

ISBN: 978-1-4834-4749-0 (sc)
ISBN: 978-1-4834-4748-3 (e)

Library of Congress Control Number: 2016903038

Because of the dynamic nature of the Internet, any web addresses or links contained in this book may have changed since publication and may no longer be valid. The views expressed in this work are solely those of the author and do not necessarily reflect the views of the publisher, and the publisher hereby disclaims any responsibility for them.

Any people depicted in stock imagery provided by Thinkstock are models, and such images are being used for illustrative purposes only.
Certain stock imagery © Thinkstock.

Book and Cover design by Asynchronous Studios.

Lulu Publishing Services rev. date: 3/10/2016

Foreward

THIS is a story of the kind of friends you can only make after dodging bullets with one another. The men and women of the ACE platoon are in transit through Kuwait on their way out of Operation Iraqi Freedom in 2004. When we find them, they are making their way to a rumored oasis on foot. To pass the time and the miles, they make a wager. Everyone takes a turn telling a story and the best of the lot wins a free meal on the rest of the group's dime. With that, *Adventures in the Fantastic* begins to unfurl.

From gangsters to medieval lore, to enraged European neighbors turning red at the arrival of new American neighbors, this modern-day frame tale gets to it all. Each soldier's story gives readers a glimpse into what they fear, what they daydream about or what they have left beind.

Through the stories, Hero, Carter, SGT Ishitani, Tom and Slim parse their words into various genres. Woven into the tales shared on the road, there is a hint of what they have to go home to—and what they don't. They talk about God and magic, morals and Twinkies, friendship and the price of a man's passions. As they walk, wonder, and wax poetic, they seem to find each other by losing themselves for a while, " ...in the expanse of dunes and a sapphire sky." Consider that foreshadowing and prepare to be immersed in these fantastic adventures.

John joined the Navy at 17 and trained as a gunner's mate. Two years later, he got out of the Navy but when the United States went to war in the Middle East, John enlisted again. This time he chose the Army. He was sent to Germany to serve as a Signals Intelligence Analyst and served in Iraq during the transition from provisional government to Iraqi government. What he remembers most from that time is being bounced around in convoys driving all over the country, and writing stories in his off hours back in Germany to help his soldiers decompress in the field.

Today John has safely returned to civilian life and has found a new way to serve others. He is back to school studying to be a registered nurse. John remains a writer and cartoonist. His work has appeared in newspapers and magazines at home and abroad. This is his first book.

Donielle Scherff

Editor-in-Chief, NOVA *Above the Fold* Newspaper
Essayist, Mug of Woe 2
Herndon, VA

For all of the people who made me think I could do this.

Acknowledgements

First, I'd like to thank my wife, Jennifer and our kids Cam and Kaity for their support and encouragement. This book would not be possible if not for the months in the field with the now defunct 501st Military Intelligence Battalion, Analysis and Control Element (ACE) Signals Intelligence (SIGINT) team from 1st Armored Division. My Mom and Dad for making me learn to read and write. Randy Hilleboe who is always willing to read another draft. Dr. David Brin for encouraging a young man who wrote him a letter about wanting to be a writer. Terry Moore for all of his encouragement in pursuing craft. Kelly Deichert for giving me a chance to hone my craft as a professional. Christian Deichert for all your support and advice. Cliff Dize, Merry Muhsman, and Donielle Scherff for reviewing these stories at different points and helping me see them with different eyes. I'd also like to thank Grace Fecteau, Jorge Quiñones, Chris Smith, Amie Smith, and Micha Beasley for their help shooting the cover photos years ago.

1

The Wager

"Only you could get trench foot in the middle of a friggin' desert," Specialist Carter said. He stood in the doorway of a 12-man tent, the air conditioned cool blowing by in exchange for the flinty, humid air of the Kuwaiti coast. His slight frame carried a heavily muscled torso, built up over a year with nothing to do but lift weights and hunt for bad guys' electronic footprints.

"Hey, bro, the ocean is less than 5 miles away, that's not exactly the middle of the friggin' desert," Specialist Hero said. She was taller than him, but a year of trying to hold to her vegetarian diet on Army rations showed.

The tent was the same dun-colored canvas as the uniforms they wore. Four apartment-sized air-conditioning units blew a steady stream of air against the 130° heat outside. The tent flap flew open again, another roll of the oppressive heat laid down across the two soldiers.

"How did I know I would find the two of you in here?" asked Sergeant Ishitani.

Sergeant "Ish" was a first-generation son of a Japanese

immigrant family in Sacramento, California. His burly shoulders belied a belly built on energy drinks and cheeseburgers. He had been able to outrun all of his soldiers before he tore tendons in his ankle during a physical fitness test on a pothole-infested strip of tarmac. Their battalion, the 501st Military Intelligence, thought before sunrise was a good time for a physical fitness test since the desert is cool. They neglected to check for other dangers, like exposed barbed wire, insurgents, or lights.

"SERGEANT!" Carter and Hero snapped to attention leaving sweaty shadows on the appropriated cots.

"At ease. Hero."

"Yes, Sergeant Ish?" Hero said.

"I heard you were on the wash racks for thirty-six hours."

"Yes, Sergeant-*ish*."

"Well, we're done and the Air Force doesn't have room for us for something like two weeks. How about you take your squad of ruffians down to the pool"

In burst the other two memebers of "heroes squad." Tom was a lanky kid of eighteen and a half. He came to the desert straight from basic and advanced training, with high school before that. Slim, a victim of Serbian adoption practices who was raised in the U.S., only ever wanted to return to his tribe of gypsies in Eastern Europe. Now he was a counterintelligence analyst and dying to slip into the shadows on the battalion's return to Germany. He already looked the part, cultivating a balance of symmetry that made him easy to forget.

"Crappo," Tom said.

"Your mission," Sergeant Ish said, is to find the pool, the food court, and the bazaar. When you do, and have had your fill, come back and report its whereabouts, understood?"

In unison, "Hooah!"

From April 2003 until August 2004, the 501st Military Intelligence Battalion of the 1st Armored Division spent a year and a half in the desert around Baghdad, Iraq. Camp Arifjan, Kuwait, was their last stop before returning to their home base in Wiesbaden, Germany. Hero, Carter, Tom and Slim were intelligence analysts under Sergeant Ishitani. In passive-aggressive rebellion, the squad used each other's first names rather than the military standard last names, except in the case of Chris Carter. For whatever reason, it just didn't feel right.

After adding 6 months to their already record length tour of duty, less than a week before the exit date, plus the bleakness of their leadership and utter lack of preparedness, most of the Battalion had lost hope. Specialist "Hero" Marshall tried to keep her squad together in the face of what felt like betrayal, by doing the right thing, whether it was the official order or not.

As part of the commanding force of the multination coalition after the invasion, they had the unique opportunity to provide transition from war to peacekeeping. They had supervised intelligence analysis that lead up to the transfer of political power from the U.S. military to the Iraqi civilian government. In reality, they faced insurgent and homegrown terrorists who fired machine guns, mortars and rockets daily. Their previous non-commissioned officer, Sergeant D., was recovering from a roadside bomb attack a month ago. Most of the soldiers came from training on how to fight the Russians, without body armor, and in trucks that had no doors or roofs. They were issued armor after reporting for duty, and made their own "humvee" doors out of quarter-inch steel plates. It was a common reflection that with some makeup and feathers, operations could serve as a set for a new Mad Max movie.

"So Hero," Tom said, "word is you got stuck on wash rack detail and they forgot about you." The squad was still acclimating to the more intense heat and humidity of Kuwait. The air had a flinty smell to it, with a hint of ocean. The breeze felt like a convection oven with the door open.

"At least I can't smell that putrid Iraqi funk anymore. That whole country stinks," Hero said. "Thirty-six hours, give or take."

"Yeah, like demolished homes, open pit sewers and decay mixed with dirt and swamp. I think I'm just going to burn my kit when we get back to Germany. They've already started releasing new uniforms anyhow. No wonder your feet are losing tread like our Humvees on that last leg."

"No kiddin'. Hey, did anyone get a shot of that fat bastard and his wing-man falling asleep at the wheel after the red zone?"

"I think Virgil did. We'll have to sneak that into the battalion video."

"Finally, one of his stories will have some shred of proof to it."

"He won't be the only one after this trip with a fair share of ridiculous anecdotes."

Everyone had a good laugh. The Battalion had pushed ahead, turning a three-day trip across enemy territory into a day and a half push that resulted in massive vehicle failure, several instances of near fatality, and general misery. Everyone in the convoy made it through to the end—including Captain D. who led the convoy in circles around the camp. He, and subsequently the rest of the battalion, was lost for six hours despite several GPS devices, as they looked for the entrance to Camp Arifjan.

"You know, that pool and complex are like 10 miles away, right," Tom asked.

With great pain on her face, Hero pulled socks over her leper's feet. "Is that a problem?"

Tom had no reply.

Slim said, "You know, boss, this is a really nice tent. You want me to hang here and uh, keep it for us?"

Hero looked around the empty tent. There were half a dozen more cots and the floors were clean. As far as she knew the battalion had not found them anywhere permanent to sleep yet. "No, we go as a team."

"It'd be nice though," Carter said.

"Oh well." Hero sighed.

The four soldiers walked out of the eighty-degree tent and into the sweltering furnace of the Kuwaiti coast. While they walked between rows of endless tenants and hastily assembled huts, the men were reminded that they had left Iraq behind them physically, but were still strangers in a strange land.

"Carter, how long do you think it'll take us, provided we don't get stuck in a circle again?"

"We're just making this a casual affair, right?"

"No need to rush, Ish didn't give us a timeline."

"Anyone else feel naked without their M-16?" Tom asked. Everyone laughed.

"About two hours, Hero."

"Then let's make it interesting."

"What's the wager, Hero?"

"There's a food court and shopping at this place, right?"

"Supposed to be," Slim said.

"Then how about this," Hero said. "Everyone takes a turn telling a story. We've got two hours, give or take. We judge the best one, and the teller gets a free meal?"

"Anything they want?" Tom asked.

"Sure. Don't be a dick."

"I'm in," Tom said, hanging back a couple steps.

"Me too, boss," Slim said.

"Was there any doubt?" Hero said.

"Then let's get it on," Carter said.

2

The Haunted Desert

HERO WAS trapped, lost in time it seemed. Whenever she closed her eyes or let her mind wander it always came back to July 4, Independence Day 2004. She left home and country eons before. After graduating college, she left for basic training, then advanced training as a signal intelligence analyst, a few short months in the freezing cold of a record-breaking German winter, and she arrived in Iraq. Immediately she pitched in to help in whatever way possible, and people forgot that she was a late arrival. She saw the betrayal within the ranks and the lack of anything resembling the Army from her father's and grandfather's stories. She kept doing the right thing, whether that's what the authorities wanted or not, and developed a reputation for it. She ended up running convoys across the country and standing more guard duty shifts than doing actual analysis. *Marshall* got used to the constant patter of gunfire outside the compound. Sometimes, she and Carter would play guitars while sitting on top of the bomb shelter by their tents, watching the nightly mortars come in. Her coolness under fire, whether enemy weapons or infighting among the unit, earned her the nickname, "Hero." Then, in two days everything seemed to fall apart.

Hero called home, only to find her once loving relationship in ruins. The next day, she pulled guard duty outside the wire rather than enjoying the nation's birthday festivities. A private was standing with her when the attack began. One second she was inspecting credentials of a CNN news van, the next she waived them off as rockets exploded feet away from her. Some nights she woke up screaming the orders to that private—"Get on the radio! Contact at main gate, unknown size, position or equipment!" Her weapon was raised and off safety before she even focused, anticipating a quick death. Nothing mattered as her life flashed before her eyes, stillness filled the void left by the realization. Then, when the smoke and dust cleared there was nothing to kill. She smoked a pack of Camels over the last hour of her shift. She sent the private to the rear. Her ears rang, she had to read lips to get by.

On the way back to her tent after her shift, she passed the remnants of the celebration by a sand volleyball court the troops had erected outside the Morale, Welfare and Recreation tents. Everyone was leaving. She thought of stopping at the phone bank there to call home and maybe find some comfort—changed her mind to keep from freaking out her Mom. She managed to get a shower before turning in for bed. When she crossed the sandy clearing between the tents and facilities to lie down in her tent, another attack hit. She could see the MWR tent in flames. No sirens blared. Helicopter gunships chased down the enemies. She applied Neosporin to her flash burns, darned her uniform where something had flown through it, and went to bed in ringing silence.

Hero stumbled on a dune. Shocked to find herself in Kuwait, she tried to keep her composure. Her men needed someone to look to. Since they couldn't trust the people whose job that was, she had to stand up. She could worry about herself after they all made it home, or whatever was left.

The sun beat down on their backs while they trudged through the sand. Wearing their issue gym clothes, wallets, water, and nothing else, it was almost too much. Carter took a long draught from his Camelback and settled into his Midwestern roots.

"I call this one, "What's On Your Mind?" he said.

3

What's On Your Mind?

BOB MUTTERED to the coach vendor in broken Mandarin. Moments later, his order for Pad Thai and shrimp translated into a heap of fried noodles and crustaceans in a pool of spicy coconut milk. The oppressive Arizona heat felt cool against the internal moxibustion of peppers and secret Asian ingredients.

"So much for the dry heat, eh?" Bob said casually.

A fellow cart diner answered, "Climate change. Didn't you hear, there's no such thing!"

They both enjoyed a good laugh in the steaming streets. A Rat rolled by on the sidewalk. *Asimov would sigh,* Bob thought. *No one makes robots anymore. The world of tomorrow ... more like the drug addicts of tomorrow.*

"Hi, I'm Jorge," said the diner.

"Nice to meet you Jorge. I'm Bob," he said. Bob waived to an Asian girl as she passed by. "Cher," Bob greeted her. "This is Liu, a friend of mine." Liu stepped up to the cart next to Bob.

"Curry chicken soup. Extra spicy," she said. "Hey, sorry I'm late."

"I started brunch without you." Bob took a pinch of his food with chopsticks. "Figured you were held up at school."

"Yep." Liu turned towards the other customer. "Hi, you work with Bob?"

Her soup came in an insulated aluminum cup, a bright green recycle reminder embossed on the side. "Thanks," she said. The server grunted.

"Just sharing the bar with your continental friend," Jorge said.

"Oh?" Liu sipped her soup. "Merde." Startled, she jostled Bob, who gagged on his chopsticks.

"Wake up!" Jorge shouted at a Rat as it recovered from hitting the cart. The caged man rattled on its way down the walkway.

Bob coughed. "Imbicile," he swore. "Not you babe."

"With all those things networked together, you'd think they could build in better controls," Jorge said.

Liu slid her arm off Bob's shoulder, steadied her cup with both hands. "Systems, right? The more control you try to take, the more errors. It's just statistics that there are a couple misses, mostly they stay on track."

"People doped up so they can live in some fantasy. Pathetic," Bob said. "At least they found a use for the addicts, thanks to Nietzsche."

Bob nodded.

"Dock workers, garbage collectors to us, Paladins and Warlocks to them," he said.

"Don't forget the informaniacs," Liu said. "Personally, I think the suits themselves are pretty cool. They make use of what would otherwise be so much human waste. Junkies get their various fixes, have a life they like and we don't do a damn thing."

"You'll have to forgive her, Jorge. She's a fan of the Raw Deal."

He ordered another drink. "New I-Dealist, eh?"

"Guilty," she said after a slurp.

"It's not all bad though. I mean, what about the transportation revolution? Buried high-power lines, harnessed for frictionless travel. You like cheap fares? That's a good thing, it looks better, reduced a lot of pollution."

"What about raildarts? Same thing," Bob argued. "Any soft metal, shove it into the pistol, and you've got a hundred rounds of little projectiles moving so fast they melt concrete. And those buried cables' EM fields only reach so high. You still have congestion."

"Only licensed guards carry them. Immediate death penalty otherwise," Liu said.

"And the mini PA engines extend transport fields, you can get over four-hundred KPH out of 'em in a normal car," Jorge said.

"While your pockets are bled dry by the exorbitant prices for those little particle accelerators."

"It goes back to Liu's Rats. The PA's increase the risk, so the compensation is for when the system fails."

Bob ordered drinks for Liu and himself. "Fails, as in riding a one-ton raildart into a congested street or building," he said.

"Okay, we'll stick to Rats," Jorge said. "The human genome industry was another revolution thanks to the New I-Deal. Wiped out poverty and welfare at the same time—"

Liu groaned. "Here we go."

"Through some offshore human experimentation and the forced contraception of drug addicts. Yeah the genetics guys did a great job. Have a baby or a biological circuit, it's women's right choose, new and improved. 'Do you have the flu, or are you making sea algae?'"

Bob winced, but held his ground. "It got population under control again. It seems a lot more humane than the decimation Asia had after there weren't enough women to stop their massive die off."

"They deserved it," Liu said. "You know they murdered us because we didn't have a penis? All kinds of crazy ways too—for generations. At least the Diaspora saved our culture, even if it bred Twinkies."

"I didn't mean—"

Liu huffed, returned to her soup. "—don't sweat it. I'm just touchy about it."

"Sorry," Jorge said to both of them.

Bob said, "It's cool. Their PR was great. Who wouldn't turn a blind eye for an end to population control and poverty at the same time? It's just that the engineers have really—"

"Babe, what do you do for a living?"

Bob stopped talking.

"What? Don't tell me he's a geneticist?" Jorge asked.

Bob said, "Non, I'm a carrier."

While he abhorred the populace-at-large and its belief in the New I-Deal, Bob was no less a part of it. Someone who could not stand working in "human services," he took a genetic courier job.

"I don't make stuff, just run data," he said.

"Oh." Jorge said, "Well, there is good and bad to it all. I've got a friend who's an Autoguard. He says it's like he' asleep on duty. Implants in his brain like sleepwalking, night terrors, that sort of thing. The corporate guys activate him when needed, like a radio controlled sentinel. He works twelve hours, hits the gym and spends the rest of his time watching sports or picking fights in strip clubs."

"Sounds lovely," Liu said.

"You're right. Some things are better for the changes."

Liu almost dropped her soup, she laughed. "Jorge, you may be getting through to him after all."

"Like the puffy sensory deprivation suits the cops use to capture guys. Or the aerosol fog they use to sedate crowds. When was the last time you heard of a cop beating some guy with a club, or using pepper spray? More effective, kindler, gentler crowd control," Bob said.

"I've been hit with that lotus gas. You just kind of walk around like a zombie till it wears off, barely know where you are," Jorge said.

"That was also the idea of the engineers. Don't want to damage their goods."

Jorge ordered another bowl of noodles. "I guess it's all about reality rights. In some ways it's just government pandering, but it works for both sides if everyone's got a right to their own reality. Of course, then you get the Rats, the eugenic laws …"

"A spoonful of sugar to help the over population go down," Bob said.

Liu dropped her cup into a nearby metal recycler. "Well guys, I'm back to it. I'll see you tonght? No quantum jobs. You don't know what they're putting in, Bob—treason, whatever. Just be safe. It was nice meeting you Jorge."

"Tonight, cher," Bob said as he kissed her.

"Peace is with you," Jorge said.

Liu replied, "And with you."

"Nice girl," Jorge said. "You're a lucky guy, Bob."

"That I am."

"So, if not a producer, then you're a courier?"

"Yeah, pays the bills and I don't have stuff growing in me," Bob said.

"Except retrovirus brain tumors."

"Someone finally read one of the brochures?"

"I work for a firm, data security. Most people don't read anymore."

Bob passed him a business card. "En Absentia. Call me if you need a drop. How do you guys beat Uncle Sam's quantum processors? If you don't mind me asking?"

"Can't tell you, it's a fluid system, but old school stuff like what you do is great outside of the building."

"Old school with new books. They can get terabytes into a few cells now with the new crypto-RNA, and it self destructs if someone messes with it."

"Yeah, Spartan tapes in the bloodstream, but bye-bye brainstem … the personal risk. How do you avoid K and R? Keep your clients from killing you after you've made the drop?" Jorge asked.

"With skin like this, it's easy to miss needle marks. At least some good came of High School. They tap my lymph nodes thought the cheek. That's the usual scratch. I try to avoid the new stuff, like quantum encryption in the optic nerve. Hurts like hell and you walk around like Odin till it's gone. Just download the genetic crap to a sequencer and I walk. That's where I'm at. If there's trouble, guys not reading the pamphlets, thinking they can make some cash on my body, I flit back to base and wait it out. They take pretty good care of me."

"And if you can't get there? Or what if the client misses the drop?"

"Retrovirus dissolves. Eats the info—"

"—and your brain," Jorge said.

"Either way, data's protected from snoops. Customers never seem to read that part though. Once in a while you get some dim wit who thinks he can use the time limit for some quick kidnap cash, or they get overzealous and think they should kill you to get rid of any loose RNA in your system. Never mind that if there was anything left, it'd kill the messenger."

"Doesn't anyone read the classics anymore? You never try to kill Hermes."

"Bro, they can't even listen to the advertising. It's there too," Bob said. He fished around in the sauce for every last morsel, wiped his mouth with his fingers and plunged them under a sanitizer. Like everyone else, his needs were taken care of as he absently paced through life.

"It's been real. Thanks for the chat, Jorge. Stay in the real."

"You bet—watch out."

Am I really so different? Bob thought, as the line of Rats passed by. Their adaptive wheeled tracks skittered over and around potholes in the massive pedestrian walk. Bob glanced to his heirloom wristwatch. *Time to pick up the package.*

The reception hall of En Absentia was an ornate diorama, the interior looked like a fantastic garden sprouted in an English gentlemen's club, framed in heavy steel and triple layers of bombproof quartz guarded by animatronic sentries. Bob entered, waved a complex gesture of fingers at the guards, and took a seat on a beautiful brown leather wingback recliner. The décor was classic Art Nouveau, an enormous simulated fireplace crackled in the air-conditioned hall. The air next to the fire was an amalgam of just-too-cold and radiant heat, based on continuous scans of his capillary blood flow. Bob pushed the technology out of his mind. He relaxed to enjoy the arcane comfort of sitting in a leather chair by an open fire.

"Drink list, sir," a hostess said.

"Chartreuse on the rocks," Bob ordered quietly. He tried to preserve the moment, " ...and a Pernod with ice, water and two sugars if I'm still here after that." Folding the drink menu up, he absently passed it to the young woman.

"Feel like a double today?" An old man in over-large black-framed square glasses sat down in a throne of iridescent leaves and thick cushions adjacent to the neighboring table.

"Sure, it's five o'clock somewhere."

Smiling, the old man leaned forward. "All the better. You get nice and comfortable. We'll call you in a little while. Enjoy yourself." He scooted off the seat, and hobbled his way back to offices behind the sheer, titanic wall that supported the steel-and-quartz enclosure.

Bob flicked his wrist. "I'd like that drink now, along with the cheese and fruit plates." *No reason not to fill up on the company's dime. That's the reason they give you a menu.*

The woman in the linen sheath saddled up to the tray table, extending hidden wings from underneath with strategically aligned triple-taps of her fingers. "Would sir care for anything else? Tea, sandwiches perhaps?"

"No, thank you. This will be just dandy."

Bob smirked politely, admired the outline of her scant boy-shorts over his drink. After he finished the snack, a green incandescent orb appeared over the remains. As if from vapor, the woman reappeared.

"You have to tell me how you do that someday."

"Company secret, sir. Follow me please."

Her slight curves swayed almost below Bob's threshold of perception as she led him on with her index finger. "In you go, sir." She laid her hand flat against the wall, a door slid aside, and she waived him through.

"Open your eyes Bob."

He complied, two sets of armatures slid into place. One pair of arms held his head and body perfectly still. The other held his eyelids open as the tips squirted saline mist onto the soft tissues.

"Comfortable?" the old man asked. His voice was disorienting, it came from all sides of the room.

"Good enough," Bob said.

"Splendid. And here's the other bit." A needle slid into Bob's cheek. Once it was extracted, a bright light flashed into Bob's left retina, followed by a direct spray of liquid onto his eye.

I should say, Argh matey, avast ye, Bob thought.

Instead he chose, "You know, I hate these quantum jobs."

"Ah, yes, but you said you could manage a double."

"So I did. Well, it must be a good one for two aperitifs and appetizers."

"Not exactly bread and water, now was it kid?" the old man asked. He stood behind him as the apparatus slid away into the amorphous darkness.

The old man held Bob's left hand and forearm, and led Bob out of the room, towards the hidden doorway to the reception hall. He passed his wizened hand in front of Bob's good eye. A series of red luminous letters and words appeared, covered in the old man's palm.

"Now, here are the addresses and times. See that you're not late to either, eh? Wouldn't want to put these nice panels to test," the old man said. He tapped his palm against the quartz.

"Of course not, sir."

"Just come back whenever you'd like to, Bob."

"I will." He headed out through the checkpoints.

Bob walked out into the bustle of city streets. Even with the pedestrians' bone-conduction implants, he still heard the sound effects, music and chatter from passerby's multitasked entertainments.

Bob pushed into the foot traffic, darted between the distracted host. "So much for doing one thing well," he said.

After a long walk, Bob made it to his first destination. *The Twin Palms Motel. It's seen better days,* he thought. He walked up to the door numbered 42. His furtive knock swung the door on its creaky hinges.

"Well, at least it isn't room 101," Bob said.

Inside were six armed guards and a fat guy in a shiny silk suit. "Welcome to my ... er, hello," the fat man said through a thick Puerto Rican accent. "My name is Rodriguez, Abraham."

"Nice to meet you, Rodriguez Abraham," Bob said.

"You taking the piss?" Abraham garbled.

"Not unless you ask to see my coconuts," Bob said through a straight face. "Or tie me up in the third room." He offered his wrists.

"You're a funny guy," the fat man said. His grim façade cracked. "I like you though. Boys?" Guards moved in like chimpanzees surrounding a monkey.

Merde. He's gonna try to take the eye, Bob thought.

"You know what I like most about you though?" the fat man asked. "You sound like Inspector Clouseau."

With that, the men forced Bob to stand still. His jaw was locked in a vice grip as his client roughed up his cheek with alcohol. "Just for insurance," he added, producing a needle. Spitting the safety cap out of his thick lips, he drew murky fluid from swollen lymph nodes through Bob's cheek. When their boss was finished, the men released him. "No hard feelings?" the fat man asked.

Innocent to the core, aren't you? I hate eye jobs.

"Naw, what's a little cheek between friends?" Bob said.

After he straightened his tie, pants and jacket, Bob walked out of the trashy apartment. He refused to look over his shoulder as he moved to the main street's curb. The nearby buildings were long past their prime.

Nothing stirs outside down here. A dust devil blew by. *Howdy, partner,* he thought. Bob laughed nervously as he watched a dog-sized rodent cross the street. He expected to see a tumbleweed roll past, but it never came. At least, not before he paged a cab.

He sorted the appointment flash, remembered the second drop's address. Bob shouted over the sitar, "Bank of America Building." The electrocab whizzed by the pedestrians and assorted quasi-motorists towards the old city center, humming along the newly buried ultra-high capacity electric cables.

Who knew that removing an eyesore would lead to mass transit? Bob mused, bopping along. *Evidently Jorge.*

What's On Your Mind?

"Okay mister. Two Euros," the cabbie said, sliding out a tray below the reinforced glass. Once he paid, the doors unsealed.

Bob stepped out into a littered sidewalk, immediately pushed and bumped by the human throng that glowed under the Arizona sun. Bob cursed in Mandarin.

Shocked faces drifted back to their diversions, a large swatch cleared for the privacy invader.

"That's better."

Bob made his way winding through the herding crowd to the bank building. The ziggurat pierced the eye line for miles, it cut through the smog to blue sky. Bob walked past colonnades of guards in the massive foyer to reach the elevators. He didn't stop his gait, even to look around. When the doors closed, he wiped his forehead. Just before his floor, the air conditioning turned on. It had little to do with the desert heat.

Almost there, Bob thought.

In sharp contrast to the Twin Palms, Bob stepped out of the rose-chrome and gold elevator into a Baroque palace.

Penthouse. I always thought it was the girls. He barely controlled a whistle as his cordoba shoes clicked against the inlaid marble floors.

"Sir?" a turbaned Sikh offered to take off his shoes and jacket.

"Bob," he said and slipped out of his footwear. "I'm fine, it's unlined." He lifted the unbuttoned breast of his linen suit.

"Very well, sir, Bob." The doorman led him into a Bauhaus sitting area. Lost in the white and black lines, Bob occupied himself trying to find a comfortable way to sit in the effete chairs.

"Bob." A businessman smiled and strode across the immaculate floor.

"I'm Jim. Can I get you something to drink?"

"A gin and tonic would be swell."

Jim snapped his fingers nonchalantly over the shoulder. "That'll be right up. Should we get down to business now, or after your drink?"

"Last appointment of the day, it's up to you." Bob tried to look relaxed.

"Oh, I see. Well, let's go for now then, shall we?"

Jim took a seat across from Bob.

"I thought that was a coffee table."

Jim chuckled as a young woman wearing a lehenga arrived with a silver tray. An ear thermometer sat on it, alongside his drink already beading with sweat.

"I don't think I have a fever," Bob said. He tried to recognize the device.

Please, no funny stuff. Just get your post-it out of my eye and let me go.

"It's for your eye. New model. Don't sweat it." Jim flashed a congenial smile. "Ready?"

Bob salivated at the sight of the cocktail. "Let's go," Bob croaked.

"Make yourself comfortable," Jim said.

The two Indians slid behind Bob, they stood silent behind either shoulder. Bob leaned forward, folding his arms on top of his knees to stabilize his head. The device's controls lit up. A programmed sound whirred while the device scanned Bob's optic nerve. When it retrieved the data, a different tone piped up. A mechanical gear clicked and the wand sprayed a mist, it smelled medicinal. The paralytic effect from encryption dissolved.

When he opened his eyes, Bob saw a green light on the stick as it was placed back onto the tray. The sight slowly returned to his left eye, giving a disorienting halo to everything in view. Like some Holy Grail, his gin and tonic glowed on the tray. Bob took a greedy draught from the sweating highball, licked his lips.

"Thank you for the drink. Everything came out okay?" he asked, taking another, more civilized slug.

"You're welcome, Bob. Now, if you don't mind?" Jim stood and swayed slightly towards to door.

"You bet." Bob checked his wristwatch.

Still early. Maybe one more? I could use some sandwiches and the rent's due. He thought of the fat man. *Never mind. I haven't even made it out of here.*

Bob slid into his cordobas in the hallway. The Sikh opened the elevator door with a bow and sent Bob down.

His eyes were drawn upwards as Bob stepped out of the elevator. The towering support structure of granite colored ceramic-polymer on the majestic ground floor distracted him from the rows of armed guards, now that his job was done. Thin accent lines of iridescent opal ran across the ribbed edges of the Moorish-Gothic hybrid arches. As thousands of glass panes caught the sunlight, the columns glowed with ethereal light. The mosaic pattern of the manufactured stone floor created an optical illusion designed to mimic pattern recognition tests. It silently teased pedestrians to solve a riddle just out of sight. It was a stunning place.

While Bob strolled out of the grand hall, he noticed one of the colonnade guards wake up and slip out of formation. Hailing an electrocab, Bob confirmed his suspicions as a private electrocar picked up the guard and followed the taxi.

He tried to think moves ahead of his opponent. *Jim? A scout? A hit? Why don't they ever read the brochures?*

"Driver, straightaway to 4156 Canberra, Higley. Use the commuter." As if Bob uttered a magic incantation, the car raised itself over the stop-and-go of the downtown to commuter traffic lanes above.

PA engines cycled, their wump-wump beat speeding up Bob's heart rate. The car joined the suspended multi-lane traffic hurtling four hundred kilometers per hour along the flat trajectory to En Absentia.

A few seconds, Bob prayed.

The electromagnetic rails lost their hold slightly as the field dissipated and the miniature particle accelerators took hold. Seconds passed in a blur of acceleration as the cab launched over the subterranean powered traffic.

What good is the cash if you're not around to spend it?

Tactics changed for the worse as the predatory town car lurched into the commuter lane from the traffic below, several spaces back as Bob watched through the rear glass. Bob piped up as he assessed his predicament. Against the howling wind and strumming engines, he said, "Give you a fifty-percent tip to drop to ground level right at the address."

"Yes sir." The driver took on the body language of a fighter pilot, computed aggressive course changes through the archaic navigation equipment. Breaking form, the money tray slid out while they were still in mid-flight. Without question, Bob dropped a hundred and fifty Euros into it.

"Ready sir?" the driver asked, with his eyes focused on the task.

"Set." Bob buttoned his jacket, sealed the pockets. The door locks popped free. As the taxi dropped roller-coaster style to the curb, Bob kicked the door open against the wind and rolled out through the opening He knocked down three pedestrians—one, a Rat, spun to wreck havoc in the mindless human tide. Bob's heart raced as he ran for En Absentia's quartz enclosure.

Bruised rib ... sprained ankle ... that elbow doesn't want to work right ...

The doors swiveled. He threw the first guard the usual complex flash of fingers, gestured a warning through the second doorway. Once there, his feet tapped against the metal grates. Bob slowed his dash to a trot. By the third door, he caught his breath. Bob spared a glance over his shoulder. An umpire in his head called out.

Safe.

"Busy day?" A young male host greeted from far across the hall.

"This is why I hate the eye jobs."

"Yes sir." The host stopped next to him. Bob stared straight ahead to watch his paranoia pay off.

Men pounded into the outer doors. A knot of gangsters was locked out on the left vestibule. A pack of Jim's muscle-bound guards streamed through the right side entrance. Rodriquez's thugs set charges against the first set of doors. Denied entry, they proposed to breech the wall. The guards gave the first interior door the bum's rush before the gangsters regrouped outside.

"Customers, sir?" the host asked.

"Not any more. They're after more than they contracted for.

Is there some way we can better advertise why they shouldn't kill the couriers?"

"The old man's afraid it would scare off customers." The host walked to his bar, so quiet Bob didn't notice.

"I guess as long as the pay and amenities keep up—"

The doors did not lock in time to block the guards' assault. The first doorman went down in a hail of their raildarts. Smears of melted flesh-tone silicone studded with black dots redecorated the marble half-wall behind his station.

The second animatron waited behind his desk for the doors to close. It allowed the men to cross between the third and second cells. In unplanned coordination with the gangsters' shaped charge's detonation outside, thinly separated sheets of quarts lanced down from the translucent crystal ceiling. The host returned alongside Bob as he watched, offered a towel and bubbling mineral water.

The host held a small try in front of him, arranged with cold packs, painkillers and a sling as he preened in the window's reflection. "Sandwich, sir? We have fresh, organic grilled eggplant with a spicy cilantro salsa, consistency of your choice. It's on rosemary Panini bread, lightly salted," he asked quietly.

They continued to observe the scene outside the final wall like an art gallery display. "Coarse sea salt? Throw a little mayo on it and I'll take two. One diced, the other puree. Thanks." Bob's eyes never left the cage, though his head turned slightly to talk to the host.

The ceiling's crystal guillotine sheets retracted in tiled order. Layers of vivisected hireling were displayed to the public in front of En Absentia's office. The gangsters recoiled in horror, dropped their next load of breeching explosives, and ran straight into waiting capture suits. Police spewed clouds of sedative gas. The fog numbed the minds of would be on-lookers. After the witnesses returned to their errands numbed with lotus gas, a policeman walked up to the En Absentia's outdoor videocom.

"Everything stabilized in there?" The tall entryway was still opaque with the menagerie of still functioning human remains. The prim host walked over to the back wall's communication unit.

"Yes sir, everything is controlled in here. One of our animatrons has to be repaired. Thank you for your concern."

"You gonna leave this one up for awhile?" the policeman said. He watched the assailants' circulation flow in awe. "It's a dandy. I heard that the Triads are looking for some couriers."

"Thank you for the suggestion. I'm sure that the doctor will want to rotate exhibits, something to match the clients' style." The host said with a smile, "Thank you again for checking on us officer."

"Peace is with *you*," the policeman departed with the department's customary slogan.

"And Service with *you*," Bob and the boy replied in unison.

4

The Duel

"SO WHAT'S bugging you, Carter?" Hero asked. She stepped out to draw the two of them away a few feet ahead.

"We're almost home," Carter said.

"And you're worried about homecoming?"

"Yeah."

Carter had joined the Army to leave a downward spiral in his life. He brought his wife Emily into the escape, left her in Germany to set up a home and a new life. Instead, she'd left him six months into the tour.

"Well, look at it this way, now that Em isn't around, you'll be able to frolic in the fields with the springtime girls when we get back to Germany."

"And if I ever go back to Missouri, there's a certain indian fella who'll want some answers on why I left so suddenly," Carter said.

"I thought you didn't want to go back?"

"It's this damned war. I don't know what I want any more. I've gotten used to just living hour by hour for what, a year and a half now? The idea of more than that is foreign and … and I've been thinking about how I might've changed. You know? Maybe now I can make that fresh start without having to leave?"

"I'll back you either way, bud. But consider the way you left things with Big Tony."

"Yeah, strippers, casino, more strippers, then getting him a hooker who laughed at his—"

"Yeah. Then you put him on a Greyhound to Branson with fifteen bucks and stone cold drunk. And he never bought your car," Hero said. "You've changed, but I doubt a thug like 'Big' Tony has."

"Hey Hero, there is an MWR tent coming up. Almost out of water. Anybody else?" Tom asked. The Morale Welfare and Recreation folks decorated their tent entrances with painted plywood cut outs of palm trees and camels.

"Yeah sure, we can go."

"How about another wager?" Carter asked.

The four soldiers pulled back a tent flap surrounded by plywood cutouts of an oasis. The sun was so bright they could only see darkness inside. Each ducked in turn, while Hero held the flap up. A middle-aged black man in a USO polo shirt greeted the men inside.

"Good morning, men," the man said.

"Good morning, sir," Hero said. "We're looking for the pool. Are we on the right route?"

"Yes you are, specialist. But you all have a long way to go. Why don't you take a load off for a couple minutes, there are vending machines over in the back, and I'll go get you all some popcorn."

"That's very kind." Hero said, "Okay, 15 minutes. Refill your canteens and do like the man said."

"And our wager," Carter asked.

"What did you have in mind?"

"I challenge you to *Battle Pong!* The winner gets a free Coke and a candy bar of their choosing."

"In that case, I accept your challenge. Prepare to suffer the consequences, dog."

Hero and Carter walked across the main tent to an open ping-pong table. A host of other soldiers, some going to and others coming back from Iraq, meandered like fish in the tank. The lights were dim, and the air was cool. You could smell the desert, under the odor of soap, popcorn, and military funk.

Like Renaissance duelists, Carter and Hero took their sides with dignity and aplomb. Raising their paddles like rapiers, each saluted the other. The ball was held out, like a cape might have been. When their eyes next met, it was with steely determination. In a blur of motion, Carter let loose the opening volley. Before it seemed to have struck the table, Hero sent a fusillade across the net at such speed Carter had to strike in anticipation rather than intentional motion. The return went wild, and struck the back of another soldier, sitting at a couch a few feet away.

Within two more volleys, a crowd gathered around at a safe distance. The paddle rapports cracked like gunfire. Their staccato beat drew more spectators while Hero and Carter began to sweat from exertion, looking all the more like their Romantic doppelgangers. After a particularly vicious volley, Hero said, "Good show, but I grow thirsty."

A deft change of angle on her next stroke sent the ball curving in a ridiculously high arc. Seizing the opportunity, Carter pulled back from the table and slammed the ball home to the edge of Hero's side. In a fluid hand off, Hero dropped her paddle from right to left hands and absorbed the force of Carter's blow. Already anticipating his win, Carter was caught unawares and dove for the short return. The ball barely crossed the net to strike the table, when the edge caught Carter in the midsection both knocking the wind out of him and his victory. The crowd fell silent. The ball lightly dribbled off of the table to bounce on the plywood floor. Hero walked around the corner to help her friend to his feet.

Amid the cheers of the crowd, Hero said, "Why don't we call it a draw?"

"Did everyone have a good time? Get plenty of water?" Hero asked.

"All restocked, Hero," Tom said.

"Good. There are about five more miles left to go, I reckon. Slim, I think it's your turn. So, let's see what all that air conditioning drew out of your brain," Hero said.

"Aw, and I thought you were saving the best for last, Hero," Slim said.

"And you can still prove me wrong," Hero said.

"Fine. This one's called 'Absolute.'"

5

Absolute

"HE'S BEEN in this latest episode for 37 hours," the attending psychiatrist said. The doctor looked over the charts, glanced at his watch. He hung the clipboard up at the foot of the bed and with a nod, left Ward with his stepmother and his friend Jose.

"Sounds like he's found something really interesting," Ward said. He squeezed Uncle Harvey's shoulder, smiled at Jose. The boys were both oblivious to Ward's stepmother.

"Ward, why don't you and Jose sit here with him for a while. Here's a little cash for something to eat later." She dabbed at her eyes while he slipped the fresh twenties into his jean's front pocket. She left, never looked back, but Ward was used to her abandonment.

Jose sat near the bed in the isolation room. "Man, it's sick that they just throw him in here."

"He did get the others pretty riled up with his talk about connecting with others in his dreams, and how we could all leave our bodies to live in the stars," Ward thought back to the scientist they had hung out in the basement with as teenagers. "But yeah, it sucks. You'd think the college could pull some of his grant money to set him up a little nicer."

"Right. A private college parting with any money would be better proof of aliens than Harvey ever had."

"Sprague's got plenty of money, it just isn't clear where it comes from."

"Maybe we should start looking beyond our understanding like Harvey said," Jose said.

"We don't have the money for the custom pharmacopeia he did, we can barely afford the stuff in the Bee Still, and besides, we've still got to pass Pimpkie's class," Ward said. "This esoteric crap would be right up old Harvey's alley if he was awake."

Jose straightened Harvey's pajama top, pulled up the covers. "I think he gets there, you know?"

"Dude, it was his claims of opening the seventh circuit that got him in here. After he was admitted, and he talked about reaching the eighth he started to go catatonic more often and for longer times. It's psychosis."

Joe's eyes stayed steady on Harvey's face. "It's real, whatever. Haven't you seen how he hasn't aged or lost weight? He's not bedridden in any way, they don't use IVs because he's healthier than you or me."

"So, of course, he's breached some magical mystery and is headed back and for the between Earth and the dog-star."

Harvey heard the boys argue over his head back in the Sprague campus hospital. "Maybe they'll wait until I get back," he said. The aborigine Harvey tried to interview would not stir from his rant, he repeated himself again.

"Darkness. Everything dims in precipitous steps."

"—what do you see, what did you see?" Harvey tried to get in edge-wise.

"Some time ago, I don't know when," the hoary headed black man continued, uninterrupted. "The world was a colored place, vibrant and full."

Harvey sighed. After a few attempts at real conversation, he just smiled as the stone-age hunter continued.

"Slowly it began to lose shape. The colors washed out first. Then the details—the enormous panorama followed by the individual minutia. Now even the details of my own self have faded away and I am barely able to recall myself. Time, position … it's all lost to me. Stuck in limbo.

"I told them not to, but they did it anyway. White people always do what they want to anyway. No respect for our ways or the dreaming. They just come in, take and take, never give or consider anything outside of their own greed or comprehension. They call us the savages …"

Harvey heard the boys leave the room, time for their next class. The aborigine man paused, turned his head and slowly acknowledged Harvey. Startled, he stuttered for a moment.

"Well, you know, I have a colleague who actually was a teacher of mine at one point. He used to say that just because science can't prove it doesn't mean it doesn't work or happen, just that our scientific philosophy has some holes in it, an imperfect system and only idiots with a few facts think that they're the end-all be-all for answers. He admits too though that he simply isn't smart enough to fix the problem, just not so self-centered that he can't admit his own weakness.

"I'm really interested in your case though. Obviously you

recognize that I don't belong in what you've been experiencing lately? Good. Do you have any idea where you are?

"Any idea what is happening to your dream? Why is it losing focus? Why are the details disappearing?"

"I have somehow fallen into the dreamtime, perhaps I am being made anew," the aborigine said. "I think it started when the white men came with their flash boxes."

"Ah, I see. And you told them not to because," Harvey said.

"Because it would steal part of my soul."

"...is the nucleus of esotetic philosophy. With that you should all be ready for the refinement and completion of your final projects. Don't forget, you have until Monday to turn them in. Fifty percent of your grade depends on it, docked one letter grade every day after."

"Looks like another study session is in order," Jose said.

"Do you have any more? My stash is gone and I'm out of ideas." Ward contorted his face in frustration at the back of Dr. Pimpkie's head.

"I know where we can get enough for tonight. Meet you in the Hall at eight?"

"Fine. I'll see if Andrea will make up some nosh for us. Make sure you come with some ideas this time too … we're in a serious crunch." Disgusted with himself and tired of projecting it onto his haggard philosophy professor, Ward moved out of the lecture hall and into the corridor bustle.

Since the boys were no longer in his hospital room, Harvey stayed in the whatever-it-was. "Dreamtime. Has a nice ring to it. Much more than 'circuit eight' or 'psycho-atomic.' Don't you think so my dear?"

"Oh yes sir. I like 'dreamtime' best," a little girl said. She appeared to be 8 or 10 years old, though dressed far too ornately for a child. She looked like a doll.

Harvey recognized her from media coverage of her gruesome death. "What's your name, dear?"

She thought about it, then conceded defeat. "I don't know. It's a funny thing, it just doesn't seem necessary," she said. "What's yours?"

"My name is Harvey. I'm a psychologist—a scientist who helps people learn about themselves. Can I ask you a few questions?"

"Okay."

"What do you remember before this?"

"I remember being on this stage, people cheering, lots of people."

Harvey was surprised to see the stage lights become brighter, fine details appeared, even in the shadows he could make out human forms.

"Really? Why?" he asked.

"Because they're supposed to, silly. I miss my Spot and Ms. Tousle though."

"Who are they dear? Pets?"

"Yes, my little dog and kitty. She's a good cat, once she ate a bug."

"That's good. Tell me, can you move?"

"No, I'd very much like to, but I can't seem to budge."

"No matter. It's not that great really. You're not missing anything good, dear."

An instantaneous flash of brilliant white light blinded Harvey.

When he could see again, the mangled body of the little girl was gone and with it the malicious crime scene he remembered from the European newspapers.

"Where did she go? Why not the others?" Harvey asked.

No one replied.

"Where did you find this stuff, hombre?" Ward said through clenched teeth.

"I know! It's totally green and shit."

"I'm already there man. Get me a pen and paper."

Jose stumbled, as he stood up and knocked against Ward's bee-shaped hookah. "Shit. Shit, shit, shit!"

Ward started to laugh. He fell over onto his side against the natty carpet. "Dude. I'm shrinking."

"Hey *guero*, you fell over. I almost killed your uncle's crazy pipe. Here's your freaking paper and pen." He tossed the legal pad and ballpoint pen down on Ward's head. Jose sat next to the hybrid hookah, released a Petri-dish like filter and refilled it with slices of Granny Smith apple. Jose closed the filter tray and tilted his head over the modified hookah's stack of filters. As the smoke drifted up, it was flavored by whatever sat in the filters.

"Sure you want to shotgun it? You might pass out again," Ward said. "Or I could get you a bunk with my uncle in the psych ward."

Jose shook his head and drew a deep breath from the column of stacked filters. The water in the pipe gurgled, the hose attachments smoked, and the room filled with a new cloud of apple-scented marijuana. "Say *'thank-you'* to Andrea for me … these ginger snaps are freaking great, man. We should get her recipe and add it into the filters for the Bee Still." Jose coughed. "Your uncle was a freaking genius man. Best pipe ever."

Ward changed out another tray in the column, dusting the damp cloth inside with a white powder.

"Okay, I'm stepping back from that one," Jose said as he fell backwards onto a loose stack of cushions.

Ward took two deep hits from the nearest hose. "Suit yourself. Nothing ventured—"

"No one gets committed," Jose said.

Ward closed his eyes. When he opened them back up, he tried to make sense of what he saw. *Why am I back in class already?*

Startled, Ward felt his blood pressure rise like an adrenaline high. It felt like his heart would burst forth from his chest. His imagination ran wild as it showered his designer t-shirt in pink mist. Ward closed his eyes again and took back control of his mind. He reopened his eyes to see the lecture hall again.

An oversized photographic portrait, set on an easel, replaced the typical three-dimensional Professor Pimpkie. The students had all turned into eight-by-ten headshots set on their otherwise normal shoulders. Ward saw his desk covered in myriad photos. Various shots from his family album—last spring break at Lake Havasu with Uncle Harvey, in the school newspaper's 4-H Club articles, other students from class were in the assorted photos too.

The spring break picture lifted off the desk in a gust of air. When it fell to the ground, Harvey began to take shape. As he stepped out of the photograph, his image left with him. An eager expression covered Harvey's face, and Ward saw pride there too.

As the wheels in his mind caught up with the action, Ward

tried to speak. "?noitcerid tuohtiw tuo dna ni seog ti, ecaps morf etarapes emit—ti teg I !yevraH" he asked.

Harvey pantomimed waking up, pointed at his ears. He seemed to say he could not hear Ward, then motioned to write down something.

I have to remember what he's about to say? Ward nodded his head.

Harvey enunciated every syllable, slow enogh Ward could memorize his words. "!tnemnrevog eht eraweB. ereh kcuts pu dne nac uoy ekawa, peels ni ereh emoC. klat t'nac ew tnereffid era setats ruO. luferac eb tsum esoJ dna uoy, draW," he said.

What the hell does that mean? Take it easy; it's this damned hybrid weed. It's sent you WAY out there. Just breathe …

A gust of wind slipped through the open classroom windows. It ruffled the pictures on Ward's desk, lifted them like fluttered newspapers in a city street. As they rose over the classroom, they began to burn. They caught the other students' photos on fire. As his photos burned, the edges of the classroom disappeared. Harvey disappeared without a trace. Other details were slowly lost—colors became muted then washed out. Ash and debris fell onto the rest of the photos on Ward's desk. As they burned, the classmates in them stood up and ran through the isles, crazed as if on fire themselves.

Jose wondered what he should do, as he watched Ward thrash on the floor. In between fits, he checked Ward's pulse and breathing. He was not in danger—he hadn't started to hyperventilate, and though his pulse was rapid, it was not dangerously high or arrhythmic. He would be fine, just worn out.

He thought out loud, "Best to eat the rest of the cookies and make sure he doesn't hurt himself. I can always do a drag-n-drop at the aid station. No one's going to turn away a clean-cut stoned white kid."

Ward came out of the trip a few minutes later, soaked with sweat. He did not miss a beat but started to feverishly write on the legal pad. Ward covered pages in moments.

"Dude, what did you see?" Jose asked.

"Shh. I've got it but …" Ward said.

Jose waited for him to finish. He said, "But what?"

"But shut up if you want to pass Pimpkie's class."

"Fine. Glad you're back," Jose said. "Jerk." He sat and enjoyed the smoke as he nibbled on the last ginger snap. The apple and cinnamon flavors blocked out most of the taste, but the smell of the raw marijuana and other things was still pungent.

PHI 431
Pimpkie

"Picture of a Thousand Lives"
by Jose Perrero and Ward Johnston

What if taking a picture really did take your soul? According to a minority theory of quantum mechanics, every choice creates a new universe. In that theory, there is a very large, but finite number of choices being made that diverges into separate universes. Some of those choices lead to dead ends, more lead back to the same outcome and they collapse onto one common universe. Other choices escape those pitfalls to create new, stable universes.

Consider a physical effect of such a diverse catalogue of events: a true rendition of events outside of time, but with their own capsule of space. Space without time, or moments frozen in time, in extenso, photographs are their own universes. Far from worth a mere thousand words, a photo is a slice of infinitely possible futures. Each image is an eternal Schrodinger's box.

Similar to *The Picture of Dorian Gray*, people continue to exist in that unknown until it is destroyed. Once no pictures are left, then that person ceases to be. When the people who remember them forget what that person looks like, they slowly dissolve into oblivion. Memories of the people in pictures who are stuck in that limbo, the people they remember are fading too, so that like the super-gravity center of galaxies, all of those people compress to infinite nothing.

Each picture is a moment frozen in time, i.e. a shot of a person at 10 years of age and that same person later or earlier are not continuous, but independent individuals. As they accumulate in the infinite, they gain more substance, but never coalesce—like amounts of the same compound, they stay independent, but grow in volume. As in our shared reality, entropy or atrophy is still constant but the more photos there are, the weaker the effects of erosion.

One logic jump away is the sum of unexplained phenomena of mankind—de ja vu, out of body experiences, past lives, reincarnation, even heaven and hell. The Absolute is not shadows on a cave wall, but pictures drawn out over time and space. God is a projectionist.

"So tell me again," Jose said. On the fold-out desk from his chair they had a notepad of graph paper. Pages and pages of words

Adventures in the Fantastic

and non-words were scribbled in the little boxes. Students milled into the lecture hall, a pall stilled their voices as they waited for judgment on their final papers. The backlog from the front settled in around Ward and Jose in the back of the room.

"Okay, second one sounds like clat ten-act-ewe, then tenor-fid era setats rue-oh."

Jose blocked out the second sentence, and stared at it. "Weird."

"Class, it's Tuesday," Doctor Pimpkie announced from his lectern. "Some of your work is already burning with a desire for the circular file." Giggles and abashed faces dotted the lecture hall in the dim, recessed fluorescent lights. The professor strutted between individual beams of track lights over the lecture platform. " ...and others seem destined for greater things." The typical front-runners sat up to receive their laurels.

"Mr. Johnston and Mr. Perrero, would you please come up here?" A mixture of astonished whispers and subtle laughter buzzed in the shaded lecture hall. Hesitant, not sure of their category, Jose and Ward nudged through the back row and approached the lectern.

Doctor Pimpkie watched the two boys step up to the podium. He said, "These two managed to find something quite interesting for this assignment. Obviously taken with some of the later ideas in class, they crafted an allegory that opens new dimensions." The old professor chuckled. "To a very old way of looking at things."

Not sure whether this was an elaborate setup to punish the slackers, Ward and Jose kept mum, blinded by the intense light they stood in. Ward kept his hands stuffed into the rough pockets of his baja while Jose seemed to gesture through his pants pockets. Visibly nervous, they cleared their throats and uttered random monosyllables.

Absolute

Doctor Pimpkie sensed their apprehension and took up the charge. "In our late study of Plato, Pythagoras, Hegel, Gurdjieff, Ouspensky, and Stiner, etcetera, we discussed secret knowledge and how philosophy and theology tackle the idea of Absolute Reality. Mr. Perrero and Mr. Johnston tied together the abstracts of these works with modern science, and found a common thread woven between them. Obviously they did not know that they would be standing in front of you today, so I trust that you will all give them respect, as I do, and at least try to understand what they wrote in their exceptional piece."

He gestured to the two disheveled students, the professor said, "Gentlemen, as the curve setters for this assignment, the floor is yours. Why don't you try to describe the basic notion of your paper?"

Ward stood in astonished silence. Jose spoke up first, "Well ... we were smo—that is, studying—in Ward's room night after night until last Thursday rolled around. We met to work some more on our project. And Ward had an epiphany." He turned to Ward and passed on the torch.

"...Right. We got really ba—tired. All of the sudden I dreamt of our classroom. When I woke up, I wrote it all down." Ward nearly lost his breakfast as his brain recombined the letters he and Jose wrote down. He lost track of his place, worried that he might fade out of the lecture hall like Harvey in the dream.

Harvey's familiar voice echoed faintly in Ward's head as he reread the message in his mind. *Ward, you and Jose must be careful. Our states are different, we can't talk. Come here in sleep, awake you can end up stuck here. Beware the government.*

Jose stared at Ward, worry plan on his face.

Ward nodded, took a deep breath to clear his head.

Jose continued on. "He was possessed. Thanks to Andrea." Coeds giggled in the shadows and brought grins to the boys' strained expressions. "Because of her cookies, we made it through the night until Ward's hand finally stopped moving. Then I typed it up and we made sense of it all. I think we were up until Saturday."

Ward picked up the narrative, "We all know what those kind of all-nighters are like." He covered the momentary lapse with empathy. Anchored again, he said, "What we came up with was an idea of why we have sporadic genius popping up in our culture, why people still believe in reincarnation and afterlife, and a lot of other really cool stuff—"

"Cool stuff indeed. Thank you gentlemen, for enlightening us on your process, if only a hint of the paper," Doctor Pimpkie cut in. "Now I know that for some of you, these two unbridled—or unrefined—minds may pose a problem because they don't sound like the officious oafs you've admired in the past. I encourage you to put aside your prejudices and read their paper. I'm posting it on the class webpage tonight. I'm even going to talk to the college's next edition of *The Thaumaturge,* get you boys some press."

Ward and Jose walked back to their dorm room after class. Once home, Jose threw a handful of frozen burritos into their microwave. Ward straightened up his desk, setting out a fresh notepad and pen next to the fan. He stepped over to the Bee Still. Harvey's warning instructions played over in his head.

"Hey man," Ward said, "remember the final straw with Harvey and the Deans?"

The microwave beeped. Jose moved the steaming pile onto

a plate, covered them in cheese and salsa, then sat down next to Ward and the pipe. They both dug in.

"Yeah, he gave 'em what for. I heard that they met out by the lava flow monument, some kind of cave or something."

"You'd believe that," Ward said. He took another burrito off of the plate, catching the drips in his hand. "What happened was, after he started collapsing in class they took him in to the hospital for observation. He was saying all kinds of stuff. Like how we could travel outside of our bodies, if we took the right drugs."

"Well shit, we knew that already. From the basement?" Jose patted the Bee Still.

"Yeah, that's one thing. Bringing it to work with you … that's suicide."

"So what's your version then, if not some weird cabal in the woods?"

"They put Harvey into group therapy and he starts telling them about these interviews he's doing while stoned, talking to people who live outside of time, in little bubbles of their own space. He demanded to speak to Sprague's President and the Deans. The assembly dismissed him as having an incurable psychosis, fixated on the sixties' claims of psychedelic enlightenment. They paid off my family to keep quiet about it. That's why my stepmom always tosses me cash and why she won't stick around Harvey.

"All of his attempts to resurrect their research were secreted away. The journals he kept of all his psychic interviews, or whatever. Even in the psych ward. Any reference to his work on psychoactive consciousness was expunged as soon as it was found."

Jose thought for a moment. "You'd think that their own reputation of expeditions into the unknown, he would've made some sense to them."

"Why would they go to all that trouble, even raiding his hospital ravings, if they didn't put some stock in it? They know, Jose. He's right, but for some reason they're keeping it under their hats."

It was widely known that Sprague College held many fruits from arcane sources. Some thought that the school was only a front for research that no one else wanted to lay claim to, but paid handsomely for in secret. Their reputation for discretion furthered the assumption, and it was reflected in the odd genius of Sprague's students and faculty.

"Jose," Ward said.

He looked directly at Ward, suddenly alert. Ward only used his name when something important happened.

"If we found a way to prove Harvey right ... Do you think they'd come after us?"

Jose closed his eyes tight, bit down against his paranoia. "They'd already be after us. Is that where the paper came from?"

"Kind of," Ward said. "I think we found something."

"You figured it out?" Jose asked. "Do you think that they'll let him go now?"

"Remember at the podium, when I almost keeled over? I solved it up there. After what he said, I'm pretty sure he's never leaving."

"What did he say?"

Greed crept into Ward's mind as he finished loading up the different filters in the Bee Still. He lit the coals with a long match and said, "He told us to watch our backs, that what we were doing was dangerous and that the government was against us."

"I knew it."

Ward blew out the match. "Well, we've been careful so far,

right?" Ward said. He set down a few extra cushions around him as smoke began to waft into the air. Ward was sly as he offered to prop up Jose with pillows against the end of the other desk. "For making lunch," he said.

Ward slowly sank from lying on his side and chatting with Jose to fall asleep with a hose near his mouth. Jose's eyes dilated and his expression drifted into numbed consciousness.

Ward was surprised when Harvey walked in. "Uncle Harvey?"

"Yes m'boy, I see you figured out the message. Sleep state everything comes in backwards too, but you unscrambled it. Knew you would, smart guy. Where's Jose?" he asked.

"I guess he's not quite up to it yet," Ward said.

Harvey eyed him for a moment. "You didn't tell him?"

"Not all of it."

"Why?" Harvey asked.

"You said it was dangerous."

Harvey smirked. "Sure it's not because you could take credit instead?"

Ward let the smile cross his lips.

"Well, I hope that in your plans you've decieded to keep me around, maybe get me out of that sanitarium?"

"Of course, Harvey," Ward said. "As long as the Man doesn't get us first."

Harvey suddenly looked skittish. "Don't joke about that, boy."

"Seriously?" he asked. "What could they do?"

"They kept me around because they can reach me whenever they want to. Dead, there's limits."

Great. Either I'm paranoid and it's coming out as Uncle Harvey, or I'm really here with him and he's freaking delusional. Of course, we're neither really here, so who's delusional? Ward argued.

Adventures in the Fantastic

"I hoped that they'd eventually recognize me as 'sane,' so I kept conducting interviews with people in limbo, but they act like ghosts—focused on their last thoughts, not exceedingly helpful."

"Is that what you were ranting about after they took you in to the hospital? Why you called the Deans together?"

"That's some of it. There's literally whole worlds out there. Entire sets of new knowledge, they don't stay as guarded with their thoughts because they think ... well that I'm the one who's not really there." Harvey scratched his head like a dog.

"You don't say," Ward said.

"I do—every mystic, every religion, they all have their place here. It's incredible. Absolution, like this little girl I met just a while ago—she's that baby that was killed by her parents? She and I were talking, then poof! she was gone like a flashbulb. Reincarnation maybe? I don't know the answers, I'm just an observer, and of course that has an effect of it's own, doesn't it?

"Now watch something really cool ..." he said.

It looked to Ward that Harvey and the dorm room were suddenly drawn away from him. Ward was outside of the increasingly two-dimensional space, his room drifted further away, left him adrift in the darkness.

Another image slowly drew near, then took on three dimensions as Ward gradually stood inside the picture. The volume turned up, so did the lights. People began to move about ward in a sea of cubicles.

Blocks of people selected parts of photos and entire photo collections for destruction. Row after row of cubicle workers burned pictures. A loudspeaker droned on, " ...is double-plus good. Future save, non-ultraviolence."

Incinerators sat at every desk. Ward was stunned and a little lost, as he drifted through the weird world. His phone rang.

Ward answered it, only to see himself staring back from the scree.

"Dude. It's like Phillip K. Dick's, *It's a Wonderful Life,*" Ward's disembodied head said. In the background of the phone's screen, he saw Jose passed out on the floor.

"Don't worry. He's listless, but alive," the head said. "Why don't you have a seat and I'll tell you all about it." Ward picked the nearest cubicle, and sat down in the wheeled dull gray office chair. There was nothing specific in the cubicle, it was the same monotonous standardized form he saw rising ad nauseum in the distance, except that the incinerator was a little too hot. It crackled behind him.

"This is the future when word gets out. If you think Harvey's nuts, this is crazy. Campaign ads on television run without real people anymore. Computer-generated people broadcast the news, they have no basis in reality and neither do the photos or videos they show, to prevent personal promulgation."

"Personal wha—" Ward said.

"Look it up when you have more time. This ain't gonna last, so just listen. All pictures are drawn and painted, but without real models—just incase. Their numbers are limited and they are burned in set orders, bound by a set of laws called 'The Picture Act.'

"Christianity became persecuted for its refusal to follow the new laws, forced to hide all of its icons and spiritual art from the international wave of equal opportunity. Islam—no graven images allowed—was valued for its forward thinking and is considered the righteous path for equality.

"But, nature abhors a vacuum. The underground now supports the artists, they generate billions of illegal portaits to help seal the souls of their patrons, that they might reach the critical media-mass and be reborn.

"God created Man, in his own image," is a political slogan scribbled in graffiti and pass-phrase for Christians and other dissidents. Time's up."

The phone went dead and everything around Ward washed out in a flash of white light.

Lights flicked on, and Ward's consciousness jerked back to his dorm. Marijuana smoke and burnt medication rankled his nose. The pungent smell blocked out the rest of the room's stale odor.

"Bro, you gotta wake up. C'mon. We can't have the police sniffing around, and you know that's gonna happen if we can't stay hinged. What the hell was that stuff?" Jose said. He swayed as he sat cross-legged on the carpet. The Bee Still smoldered with a final puff. Jose watched Ward regain consciousness through bloodshot eyes.

I get it now Harvey. I'll fix it, Ward thought, barely able to anchor himself in reality.

Ward mumbled, "Turn on, tune in ..." His thoughts were hazy, not sure of anything his body said. He sat up, turned on the nearby desk fan, then threw up in the trashcan under the desk.

Jose crawled over to Ward, patted him on the back. He sat a bottle of water within reach as Ward lost his balance and fell over with the trashcan. "I saw it too," Jose lied. "You want me to write the paper?"

"Thanks bro, but I got it. You just do the edits and next

version. That's fine." Ward knew Jose's offer was a bluff, but covered for his pride. He took several deep breaths of the cleared air, fumbled over his head for a notepad and pen from the desk, and began to write the next paper. "It's like the next step, struck by genius … like Harvey said, psychic critical mass, media mass. Absolute Reality."

Jose picked up the dishes and the filters from the Bee Still. He walked down the hall to the bathroom, washed them out in the sink. Finished, he pushed open the door with his foot, his nose rankled in the hallway.

"Shit," he said. Smoke drifted out from their room's open door.

Jose dropped the dishes to the floor with a clatter. Doors began to open as gray smoke clouded the lights in the dorm hallway. People scurried around Jose as he passed. He slid into the room with a crowd at his back.

Ward was gone.

Someone pushed him aside, burped a fire extinguisher across Ward's desk and sent a few extra squirts into the already smoldering trashcan next to it. With the fire out, Jose fell onto the trashcan.

He dumped its contents onto the carpet. Inside were all of the notes and the drafts of the first paper, destroyed, ashes. He pushed himself up with a hand on the desk's chair, wiped the foam off on his cutoffs. The floor's RA ran into the room.

"Jose, are you okay? Where's Ward?" she asked.

"He's gone."

"What do you mean, he's gone?" She looked around the room, frantic that Ward had died in the fire.

"He's not here," he said to assure her.

Fears allayed, she assigned taskes to the crowd. It quickly dissipated. "How did this happen? Where is Ward? What was in the trash can?" she asked.

Jose clamed up, looked around the floor and trash. His eyes found his soiled cutoffs. Gray ash was mixed with the dried foam from pushing himself up off the chair. He mumbled, "Erased."

6

Cracks in the Armor

"BOSS, DO you think we're ever going to leave this stinkin' desert?" Slim asked.

"If you'd asked me six months ago, I probably would have just toed the party line."

"And now?"

Carter distracted Tom to give them some room.

Hero lost herself for a moment in the expanse of dunes and sapphire skies. "After Independence Day's attack?" Hero shifted her feet, in limbo between thoughts. "Now? Now, I have no idea what's going on. That's the honest truth."

"I meant, are we ever going to make it to the pool?"

Hero laughed. "I know, right?"

Carter chimed in, "Hey boss, did you ever finish Dune?"

"Only the original set."

"What I wouldn't give for a still suit about now," Tom said.

"I can arrange it so you drink your own sweat, if you want," Slim said.

"I think he does enough of that around Sergeant Ish," Carter said.

"Yeah, so why aren't you looking like Arnold?" Slim asked.

"Sorry the steroids make me deaf."

Slim pushed Tom. Carter pushed Slim.

"Funny, I thought you were the unlicensed pharmaceutical retailer, Slim," Hero said. She saw a flut of occupied lawn chairs under a tarpaulin awning two hundred yards away take notice. "Let's see, who's next?"

Stumbling in the sand, Tom said, "I'll take it, Hero."

"First time he's volunteered in months!" Slim said.

"Knock it off, Slim. We've got an audience. Unless you'd like a detour and some forced volunteerism?"

"Whatever. It's my turn so shut it. It's called 'Trees in the Forest.'"

7

Trees in the Forest

"PULL UP your cloaks and stand very still," Arjin whispered. He scanned the massive rock formation in the forest clearing. His head tilted, golden eyes focused on a single point. "Trolls," he said. From across the clearing's expanse he saw an enormous pile of boulders jutting out of the dense groundcover and dead leaves.

"That big, gray boulder on the right moved," Gilesh said.

Moine stood straight, like a willow. Her dark brown hair draped over her shoulders in fluid waves. Against her bright white skin it looked almost black. Gilesh snapped a twig underfoot as he planted himself. Startled, the rock trolls tossed helmet and shield-sized stones the quarter league across the clearing.

"Do not move," Moine said, under her draped hood. "They will forget soon."

Howling, thrashing, the males of the troll troop shook their bodies at the empty forest. Soon their posturing turned to self-congratulatory whoops and back-slaps. The trolls returned to eating lichens and grubs. Their mottled skin dissolved into the shape of rock faces and nooks.

"Where did they go?" Gilesh whispered, as he watched the boulders.

"The same place we did," Arjin said. His body moved with the exact grace of a mountain lion. Thews hardened from years of forest life slid gracefully under sun-darkened skin. He took Moine's hand, she took hold of Gilesh's free arm in her other. Strung together like beads, they slipped deeper into the thicket of wispy leafless trees. The bare branches scratched and tugged at the cloaks. Gilesh's cowl crept back and gave the twigs space to slap his face.

The baby fat in his cheeks, tousled yellow hair, and his light blue eyes belied his skill as a spearman. His innate fighting ability was paradox to his youth and lack of experience. Thorns on a branch raked his jaw. He wiped blood from the scratches. Through clenched teeth he said, "Ow."

Arjin looked around after they were well hidden by the mass of thin trees. "All right, we should be well covered here. Those, my young warrior, were rock trolls. They like all manner of filth and entrails. I'm sure they'd love to sample your delicacies. Men don't come through here much. I think the trolls consider them a rare treat."

"Oh. Lovely. So we travel through the forest to avoid detection, only to be eaten by forest creatures? Brilliant idea, sir," Gilesh said.

"Relax, Gilesh. There is no finer woodsman than Arjin. He just saved your life against an immense foe."

"What, by standing still?"

"Thank you m'lady. Yes lad, by standing still. Look at the cloak you wear. The mottled grays and browns with untidy black

Trees in the Forest

lines. No thick bits, all fine lines, all going the same way. Now, look to the route we just came."

"I can't see the boulders," Gilesh said.

"What about the distance we've just come?" Arjin asked.

"I cannot judge it. The branches all come together in a haze," Gilesh said.

Two more fist-sized rocks crashed through the trees just behind them.

The trio stood unaffected. "Precisely. Throw your cloak on, stand still, and from a few dozen paces you become the entire thicket. Use your environment to the advantage against numbers, son.

Speaking of cloth, did you get what I asked for, Moine?"

"Yes, a remnant of purple silk. The smith kept trying to settle me on gold or silver pins instead of the steel, and the stonecutter was a pain. Kept wanting to set the citrine buttons in a ring or bracelet."

"Well, it would be harder to wear as a shiled with all that wrapped around," Arjin said.

"For what, a mouse?" Gilesh asked.

"A pixie," Moine said.

Arjin took up the march again, his feet barely rustling in the fallen autumn leaves. "We are nearly to the old castle," he said to Moine.

"Good work, Arjin. Even my Duke is afraid of the Sorcerer."

"He's good reason to be. The Sorcerer is the most powerful magician left in the Pfalls territory, counterpoint to our dear Duke's appointment to rule by gods' will. He is also very old. Those two things put together to make the boots of any tyrant quake."

"The Duke is not a tyrant," Gilesh rebuked. "He's devout and made of iron but only for the betterment of our people."

"Don't," Moine said.

"What? How can you not support your Duke as a bound concubine? I know it was a political arrangement with the forest fey, but surely you see his justice?" Gilesh asked.

"Justice is a popular term for holy writ," Arjin said.

"I wouldn't expect you to understand the ways of the court, coming from the forest," Gilesh said.

"Raised and adopted by pixies, yes. Yet I come from the courts, a higher station than your lineage, boy, though you may be too young to know the tale."

"And you don't yet understand the balance of these lands, Gilesh," Moine said.

"How can you want to limit the Duke's righteousness? Isn't that best for the people?" Gilesh asked. He was engulfed in piety. Moine and Arjin looked tired.

"What happens to a cooking fire if you build it too high?" Arjin asked.

"It cooks faster?" Gilesh replied.

"It burns the food, the pot, the cook. It spreads to the land. Everything is engulfed by the flames. A cooking fire that burns too hot fails to nourish. It wrecks havoc and death instead. So it is with a ruler and his territory. That is why we are here—to ensure the land survives."

"I still don't understand why we're here. The Duke has taken care of the situation. He campaigns against traitors as we speak. We should be fighting the enemies there, with him. A company of men was dispatched a week ago to parlay with the Sorcerer."

Trees in the Forest

"Have they yet to return?" Arjin asked. "They are likely all dead. The Sorcerer has been lured by the promises of evil. Now he poisons the land and the Duke's fire burns the rest."

"Moine, can you not convince Arjin of my point? Surely, as a Princess of the Fey, you can see how the Duke is defending our territory, preserving justice for his people?"

"I love our Duke, Gilesh." She looked up at Arjin. "I have given much to help him and to serve the people. I continue to serve, even if without his consent."

Arjin did not bother to respond. His hand trailed under his cape. Moine reached for it, squeezed for a brief moment as if thrusting momentum into her step up the rocky terrain.

"Watch your step," Arjin said. "This is my old home. There are more than rock trolls here. We should encounter my family soon. I haven't been here in a long time."

"And that means blood," Moine said.

Gilesh stopped mid-stride. "What?"

"Pixies. They are a little more ferocious in disciplining than humans—drawing blood is how they settle slights," Moine said. She hiked up her skirts to clear a rock up the hill.

"Fiends," Gilesh said, under his breath.

Arjin smirked. His ears twitched with effort as he listened to the forest. "I can only show you what to do, Gilesh. The learning part is up to you. I was taught their way." He gestured to scars on his cheeks. One stood out, raised above the rest, a finely carved sigil under his right eye. It shone with a light of its own when he touched it. "You won't be of much use, other than as a foot soldier, if you can't get around prejudices like that."

"I didn't—"

"Yes, you did." Moine cut him off. "Just because I am the Duke's Lady doesn't mean I don't also owe allegiance to the forest."

"Does that include the Sorcerer?" Gilesh asked. He blushed in embarrassment, at the same time his anger rose in outrage.

"Not if he decided to abandon us, as seems the case," Arjin said. His eyes roved the leaves of the trees.

"And you would kill your friend?"

"You think me duplicitous? Treasonous? The Sorcerer is no one's friend if he has tilted the balance. Our duty is to the people—especially the Duke's. Never forget," Moine said. She locked eyes for a moment with Arjin.

"If he chose evil, can he not choose good again?"

"That is what we will see," Arjin said. As they crested the hill, castle ruins came into view. Still a ways off across the hilltop, the giant stone bedrock of its foundation rose out of the forest detritus. Signs of a recent encampment littered the tree line in front of them.

"Where are the Duke's men?" Gilesh asked. Several stumps sat, gathered around the charred remains of a large campfire. Scattered remains of an animal and crockery were strewn from the charred coals as if the pots and rack had exploded.

"So, do you use powers to track them from here? Some kind of divining?" Gilesh asked.

"That's not my gift. I can track because it meant food as a child. The fey gave me forest abilities to even the odds, after they adopted me."

Gilesh shifted his eyes to Moine.

"I'm not putting on a show for you, Gilesh." She caught Arjin's eyes and he smiled. "I did that once and it went badly."

Arjin stifled a laugh.

"Not to mention that the pixies will find us soon. When they do, they'll be more upset if we're crossing that magical line for no reason but laziness," she said.

"Don't you dare call them fiends though, boy. They aren't malevolent, they educate by tricking others. They're like protectors here, but the rules are of the wild forest—not your court niceties," Arjin said, he touched his scarred cheek. "No way to be sure if that's mess or—" Arjin squatted down by the fire. A hum of wings grew closer.

"Oh, it's 'or' alright, you malformed elf." A tinny voice buzzed.

"Swat, but do not crush." Arjin said, as he drew his cloak tight. Moine and Gilesh pulled their hoods down.

"What? Too good to do real battle with the likes of us? Are we merely bugs to you? Pesky insects?" A swarm of pixies dropped on the party from above, tore at their cloaks and pulled at the bunched folds around the fronts.

"Anatoliah, is that you? Still Queen, I see. It's been ages." Arjin said. A golden clad goddess in minature hovered before his face. Blue ribbons laced around her body, tails flapped in her wake. "The blue is a really nice touch. New?"

She raised a hand, her company halted, frozen in place. Some had their needle-sharp teeth sink into fingers just under the others' cloaks.

"Get off!" Gilesh cried out in surprise more than pain. He tried to shake a couple biters off. Blood ran in small rivulets down his hands. "Nasty little vamps." Gilesh shook his hands trying to throw the little people off. The pixies obeyed the Queen's command and held fast like bulldogs locked in mid-attack. Gilesh danced around like a mad drunkard.

"Queen, I cannot concentrate if your guard continues to pester the boy. I beg, for all our ears, will you let him go?"

The pixie waived her hand, as if dusting pollen off her ribbons. The guards were quick to dodge Gilesh as they released him. He tried to burn them to cinders under his embarrassed gaze. The few on Moine and Arjin held fast, neither paid them any attention, focused on the Pixie Queen.

"Yes. The ones who came before you. They did not know our rules." The Pixie Queen gestured towards the fire pit.

"I bet you educated them well. I still remember my lessons."

She pulled in closer, touched Arjin's cheek where a magic sigil had been cut in fine line detail years ago. She licked her lips. The Pixie Queen said, "So do I, oaf."

"Moine, if you can, please pass me the roll of purple silk I asked for earlier."

She complied, covered in pixies like glimmering flowers. Arjin passed the roll towards the Queen. "Here is tribute for you—steel pins, arms made for your warriors, and a citrine shield for my golden goddess." He held out the unfolded package for her inspection.

"The silk is from my own collection." Moine said, "It would make a fine bed, or coverings for your chambers." She looked at Arjin, a shared memory passed between them of younger bodies and forest glades.

"Yes Moine, I see that too. Don't forget that I remember you. You used to love to play with us as a child. What happened?"

"Actually, that's what we've come to see the Sorcerer about," Arjin said.

"Ah yes, the Duke," the Queen said. "The Sorcerer and the others are inside."

The pixies let go with little suction noises. Moine held out a dripping finger, a female lit upon it sitting in the blood. The Queen nodded in approval. "No harm but my own," Moine said.

The pixie wrung her hands in a series of gestures. Moine's blood turned to glittering dust and fell from her. Other guards drifted through the magic, some swooping up to lift long strands of her hair and float in the air.

"We must attend to our friend," Arjin said. He knelt in front of the Queen. She transformed his wounds and pollen fell from his body.

Gilesh was dive-bombed by several guards with acorns. "Get off, bugger." His wounds sealed but the blood stayed still in his shirt cuffs and crusted on fingers. High pitch laughter followed him as he joined Moine and Arjin toward the ruins.

As the trio moved out of sight, the Pixie Queen whispered, "You may be too late." Tears stained her cheek under her pitiful warning. The doom on her people complete, their queen burst into ethereal green flames. She fell as ash to the ground and her people scattered in panic. Their treaty of silence was broken.

"Gilesh—up front. Shield and spear. I'll come on the left with sword. Moine, cover our rears." Arjin dropped the hand he held under their cloaks.

"I'll kindly ask you not to be so familiar with her, sir. Moine is the Duke's concubine. She should be protected, not a defender."

"Indeed. I apologize, young sir. I was not aware that you wanted her to remain in the magic of the forest alone, possibly open to attack by these men. Madam, if you would be so kind."

"Gladly," she laughed.

Embarrassed, Gilesh took up arms at Arjin's side. Gilesh did not see the glittering droplets and ephemeral glow from Moine's lily-shaped sleeves.

"Shall we?" Arjin asked. They shuffled up the open stone stairs through the first arches into the ruined castle's grounds.

Inside were long, dark hallways of heavy stones and slit battlements. They climbed up the sloped corridors. There was an odor of disuse inside—dust covered everything.

"It is too dark, Arjin. I cannot see. We could be surrounded."

"You're right." Arjin mouthed unspoken words in the twilight cavern. He threw a thumb-sized piece of quartz into the air in front of them and it burst into radiant light. It illuminated the chamber like a torch. They saw cobweb covered suits of armor that lined the column strewn hall. The team pressed on.

A sudden breath of old dirt and rot raised Arjin's hackles. "Necromancy." It grew stronger as they continued into another dilapidated courtyard. Gilesh's spearhead quivered in the air with his nervousness.

"Stand ready," Arjin said.

The press of the rotten stench tried to overwhelm them. In the shadows drawn by Arjin's light and the passing courtyard, feet rustled. Breathy consonants streamed out of Arjin's lips, the light grew brighter. The shambling creatures were caught off guard, suddenly visible.

"Cut them down!" Arjin cried, as he drew a thin, flat bladed sword and a hatchet from under his cloak.

"Undeads," Moine cursed. A wave of her hands created a shield around the group. "You can come and go through the bubble. They cannot reach you within." All hope for reconciliation with the Sorcerer was lost. She gazed through the ephemeral blue light of her spell. Her heart sank as she confirmed her fear. "All those men."

"Gilesh, you still waiting for your Duke's men?" Arjin asked.

"Are they here?" His eyes were wide with joy.

Arjin threw shards of cleaved tunic towards the boy as he swept his spearhead through necks like dandelion stems. "The price of your righteous piety."

Gilesh's spear cut a swath further into the hall. Mangled bodies groped headless at his feet. Dismembered torsos heaved with unnatural vigor on the floor while their separated arms sought out ankles to climb. Moine and Arjin followed, her shield blocked their flank as Arjin finished off what the spear knocked aside.

Sunlight filtered in through the end of the hall. "Almost out of here. Will they follow?" Gilesh asked over his shoulder. More undead bodies filed in from sidelong passages. They began to overwhelm him as his spear shaft was wedged into the crowd.

Arjin roared, thew himself bodily into the fray. He used the spear as a guide, cut down bodies on either side as he ducked left and right under it. His arms flailed as their strength waned. The hatchet became a bludgeon, crushing bones with sheer force of his blows. They emerged from the hall as a burst of rot showered the large courtyard flagstones. The Duke's former men trailed them, but in the light their animated limbs fell still as the dead. Moine's shiled dissipated.

"What walks in shadow cannot stand in the light," Gilesh quoted.

Arjin slapped his shoulder to warn him. "Keep up your guard. Leave the Duke to his piety. More lurks here than his dead soldiers.

In front of them stood an elaborate façade of white stone, bas-relief and gold gilt. Niches covered the face. Their arches supported a massive balcony four tiers above the courtyard and a heavy, peaked roof further up. In each of the alcoves were elaborate carved sculptures.

A low rumble built up in the air, the ground trembled. Rocks tumbled and cracked along the courtyard's carved decoration. A faint undulating chant echoed from the portals opposite them, under the façade. Arjin narrowed his gaze as he searched the openings for the source. He locked his eyes on the far right of the edifice. A portcullis crashed down, dug into the stone floor. A heavy, iron-bound wooden door slammed to in front of it. The quake's ferocity shook the entire courtyard, heaved the flagstones. A few columns tore loose, crashed to the pavement.

"He's got rock trolls along the ramparts," Gilesh said. He pulled his cloak around him, then released it. "I doubt the cloaks will help us much here?"

"Not so much, but you're catching on. Just move slow and steady, try not to step on anything breakable," Arjin said. He turned to the side, towards Moine. "Do you feel it?" Arjin asked.

"Could they be here just for the ruins? They're not taking any interest in us …" Gilesh whispered.

"In my very bones." She closed her eyes, pointed through the left most bottom niche. "It's intoxicating."

"What is?" Gilesh asked.

"Evil," they said quietly.

"What happened here?" Arjin asked. He stared at the façade.

"I've never seen it before either." Moine said, dividing her attention. "This is no court hall. This is—"

"A Sorcerer's sanctum," an otherworldly voice announced. The sound echoed off of the courtyard sides. "My late friends."

"Don't you mean, old?" Gilesh asked.

The Sorcerer said, "Not for long."

The main statues in the tower's niches were shaped after men, with grossly oversized dimensions. Kings matched with the icons of their reigns—bristled weapons, magical talismans held aloft, physical bodies that never appeared on their forefathers. The statues in the tower came to life. They moved as if the stone was as pliant as flesh, though from the effects of their bodies on the tower, no skin was ever so tough. The stone warriors scurried down the front like lizards. They defied the bounds of men in the angle of their attack. Stone men arranged themselves phalanx fashion on the edge of the courtyard. With a coordinated grunt, they stomped towards the threesome in lockstep.

The noisome activity drew the trolls' attention. Shards of balustrade and architecture hurled into the formation, knocked aside the animated statues. The enchanted stone men did not recover after they were struck.

"Break their skins," Moine said. Her eyes burned brilliant, lit with magic. "They are meant to intimidate. They strike when you are paralyzed in awe."

Snakes and creatures, imps and stone birds came to life out of the frieze borders around the court. Trolls hurled whatever they could find into the morass. They had no particular target, just whatever moved. One by one they dropped to the gound and did battle hand to carven hand in the courtyard. The phalanx marched steadily onward. The myriad small creatures moved in a faster wave, as they slid and ambled across the broken floor. They drew a noose around the adventurers.

"Move toward the door on the far right of the tower," Arjin said.

Gilesh held his spear lance-fashion under his arm, always aimed toward the face of the tower. Arjin was their eyes as they moved back to back toward the gate. The phalanx halted, just out of Gilesh's reach. One of the statues blew through a carved horn and the smaller host sped their way from the rear, toward Moine.

"I have to conserve," she said.

"Gilesh, take point," Arjin said. He switched to face the onslaught, handed his hatchet to Moine. "Just crack and chip?"

In her hands, the hatchet grew to the size of her leg. "Should work," she said. Swung like a croquet mallet, she sent an imp careening into a knot of creatures. Their stone broke and lay lifeless in a heap. Trolls howled in the rear echelons, dumb to the trio's presence.

Gilesh's spear sang against the skin of the defenders as the phalanx blocked their way to the door. The warriors pressed in behind a row of carved shields. "Help!" he cried.

Moine came alongside Gilesh. The shield slid over them as the phalanx joined the fight. Arjin filled his left hand with stone shards and took off his belt. He whipped the two ends into his palm, formed a sling with the leather and began to sight in on the stone beasts. They knocked into one another with the projectiles. It decimated their front ranks in short order. Trolls rolled in to secure more stones to battle the statue warriors.

"It sounds bad, but I'm out of rocks," Arjin said.

"We're not getting much here," Gilesh said. He ducked, the shaft of a spear cracked against Moine's shield.

"I don't know how long I can keep this up and still fight," Moine said.

The Sorcerer whispered with the force of a battering wind, "Better here than in the tower, Princess."

"That's it. We have to push," Arjin said. "Run!"

They dove through the shield. Moine trailed its edge behind her, confusing the simple trolls and giant stone men alike. The phalanx attacked the blue glow as it wove between and around them. The trolls continued to tear into the statues. As if their collective leader reassessed the objective, the stone men turned to focus on the trolls. It provided a distraction from Arjin's desperate bid for the alcove's door.

"We can fight them off using the doorway as a funnel. You can use the time to recoup," Gilesh said.

"Do it, Moine."

Moine threw up her arms, her sleeves spilled golden dust in a trail. The light burned brighter as her sleeves slid back to the elbows. Molten fire consumed her forearms, her hands encased in impenetrable light. Arjin distracted Gilesh's stare with a hand on his back.

"Close your eyes boy," he said.

Thunder shook the ground as she clapped her arms over her head. A cataclysmic ball of light exploded across the courtyard, burned all of the Sorcerer's minions to dust. Moine shone with an ethereal glow. Her gown transmuted into a shimmer of white and gold. The men regained their feet and moved towards the fortified door.

"If he didn't want us to come in, he would have made more doors to choose from," Arjin said.

"You're not walking any more," Gilesh said.

Moine glided across the upturned stones, her feet invisible under her skirts.

"This is the reason she's here. Keep quiet," Arjin said.

The door tried to blend into the façade, but Moine caught it with an outstretched palm and slid the illusion away. She drew her fingers into a fist in the air. The gate tore off its hinges. The portcullis crushed into nothingness as they approached.

The Sorcerer spoke from the shadowy depths, "Ah, the Fairy Princess returns. Anatoliah was right to remind you before you entered, dear. Now a true battle begins."

Arjin yelled, "Did you think we were here because of a man who cannot control his passions?"

"We knew something awry, something magical," Moine said. "Only necromancy would make the man appointed to rule by the gods go so far. The world lies in balance between the forces of light and dark. When darkness grows, light must increase in its own severity."

"Men are fools not to see the oracle in their homes," the Sorcerer said.

"Indeed," Arjin agreed.

"So you fight to make your Duke darker?"

"Rather, restore sight to him. Because of you, he shines so brilliantly he blinds himself and the whole land," she said.

Arjin threw a shard of quartz down the hall. The magic ignited, burning the crystal white-hot. The Sorcerer detonated the suspended light and showered the trio in small sparks of sandy fire.

"Please tell me that isn't all you brought to the fight," the Sorcerer said.

"We all choose which side we're on. It's changeable. You used to be a friend, on the side of good," Moine said.

"Be true to your nature," he said. "This is mine."

"Very well. Moine, if you wouldn't mind?" Arjin slid off his gloves, onto a belt clip.

"Blessed be," he whispered. Moine's body threatened to swoon. Her magic became palpable as it probed against the Sorcerer's amorphous barricade in the twilight of the hall. Darkness enveloped them. It ate the light. A preternatural sensory deprivation surrounded them. Moine's luminescence grew. Her light poured over Arjin. His bare hands dug into the stone floor. Gilesh's eyes roved through the the impenetrable black. The stones gave way under the Arjin's palms. They cracked with upturned soil. It smelled like life, a dark musty potential for growth.

"Gilesh, have your spear at the ready."

The Sorcerer's voice boomed in the antechamber, "I told you, it would have been better for you to be crushed outside than to die in here, Moine. You and your friends. Tell me, Arjin, what would you give to have your Spring Maiden back with you, running free in the forest again?"

"Not as much as you traded for this," Arjin said. "You knew that Anatoliah would not give in to you, other than to serve her people. You taught me that was the way, years ago. Did you burn her because of me, or was that inevitable?"

"It was you. You were her people and not, at the same time. Your ambiguity killed her. She set this in motion when she adopted you, Arjin. The wilderness of the forest is the balance to man's crude fashion. She crossed the line bringing you in, as did your sweetheart when she forged an alliance with the Duke."

Gilesh found his voice. "For the greater good," he said. He choked and could not speak. Moine's luminescence waned, then exploded. What was probative became violent force as she drove the Sorcerer's power back. A man's shadow lay black on the far wall of the chamber. Arjin pulled Gilesh to the ground, he gasped for air and caught his breath again. Overhead, Moine focused her energy into that darkness, pinning it to the wall. She forced all of his power back into that shadow.

Moine collapsed on top of Arjin and Gilesh. The shadow crawled up the wall and spread across the ceiling.

"She's not breathing," Gilesh croaked. "No heartbeat."

Arjin laid his hands over her heart and cradled the back of her neck. He ignored the recovering Sorcerer and blew breath into Moine's lungs. Between breaths he said, "Spear."

Moine's body caught with a gasp.

"We're not done yet, Spring Maiden. I need your light," he whispered in her ear.

She sat up next to Arjin as he dug his hands deep into the earth again. Green things sprouted between Arjin's fingers. The stones of the floor heaved as massive vines coursed up from the fecund earth.

"Plant it." Arjin said, a smile on his lips.

Gilesh put all his weight into driving the butt of his spear into the center of the tendrils. Swiftly, the growth took hold of the shaft and locked it in place. Gilesh dropped down to his knees and they linked hands. Moine drew fresh strength from Gilesh's youth, her light grew to feed Arjin's tendril tree as it sought out the wizard's corporeal form above.

Vines formed knots in the descending darkness. The Sorcerer said, "You cannot bind me so easily, Arjin." The weight of his magic was a vise, meant to squeeze the life out of his would be assassins.

"Magic is still nature," Moine said.

"Now!" Arjin yelled.

Moine's light blinked out. Bodies collided as they dropped to the ground around the base of Arjin's vines. The crushing darkness smothered them, but wet sounds whispered across the abyss like dawning rays chasing back the night. As the Sorcerer's assault receded, the scent of blood pierced the void. Light shone down from high, slit windows in the far wall. It pooled around Arjin's vines as they formed into a small tree and absorbed the body of the dead man. Gilesh's spear formed the trellis that shaped the trunk. Boughs pressed against the roof and reached for the sunlight through the wall. The steel head of the spear reached out from the branches, covered in black gore.

"Success, such as it is." Arjin rolled back from his haunches onto his feet, dusted his hands off. He offered help to his comrades.

"Pity," Moine said icily.

"Maybe it will stem the tide here."

"Maybe," she said.

"People choose their own paths. We all know that. Evil doesn't change things—it only brings them to the surface."

"I still liked it when we couldn't see the horrors that lurked around us," Gilesh said, unable to pull his eyes away from the dead man spitted on his pike until his body was engulfed.

He tuned towards the door, saw Moine draw back from Arjin's silhouette, her hand stretched out to his cloak.

"Should we head back now?" he asked quietly.

"I don't want to be around this smell any more than we have to," Moine said.

Gilesh walked around them and headed towards the door.

"That's not rotting flesh," Arjin said. His body tensed. He sprang and wrestled Gilesh to the floor. A massive fist crashed on top of them. Arjin's momentum carried Gilesh clear of the rock troll's blow.

"Get clear!" Moine shouted. Her hair streamed back from her head as the air charged with power. Gilesh leapt for the abandoned axe, drew his cloak around him from reflex. Thunder detonated inside the small chamber. Gilesh's ears rang and he felt blood drain from his ears, nose and eyes. He jumped.

Moine crumpled where she had stood, hidden in the fine lines and mottled colors of her cloak. Drained of her magic, it returned to its former dullness and camouflaged her between the stones and tree limbs.

Light streamed through the broken holes in the far wall. Gilesh went berserk, wielding the axe like a mace, as he smashed with unrelenting fury into the beast. He circled behind the animal so that there was no escape. He beat it savagely towards the broken wall. Wet slaps and gurgled howls overcame the ringing in Gilesh's ears as he butchered the killer. The immense troll staggered, collapsed against the tree, but Gilesh drove onward. He carved great rifts in its belly, hewed pound after pound of flesh from its flank. Driven from the tree's support, the troll braced itself against the eroded wall. Under the creature's weight, the damage to the wall was finished. It crumbled down the sheer cliff outside and took the troll with it.

Gilesh fell to the ground and vomited. Covered in blood and gore, he crawled to the heap covered in the mottled cloak. Moine stirred.

He gained his feet and wretched again. Gilesh staggered over the slick rubble to Arjin's body. "What more was there to know?" he asked.

Moine hobbled over to him.

"Learn your lesson well, Gilesh. He showed you everything you need to know."

"I don't understand, but I know."

Sunlight engulfed the Sorcerer's tree, open to the western horizon. "It's a beautiful valley," Moine said.

"They were friends?" Gilesh asked. He gathered Arjin's body on top of his cloak, in as dignified repose as he could.

"A long time ago. He brought Arjin back to the courts."

"Then, maybe, this is where they should stay? A foot in each." He took two corners of Arjin's cloak and began to drag him around to the side of the tree that faced the valley. Moine joined him, lifted the corners by his feet. The tendrils reached out for him, as if they recognized his familiar power. Moments later, the tree mummified Arjin within its roots.

8

The Interloper

"NICE ENDING, yo," Hero said.
"Glad you liked it at least, boss."
"Looking forward to some of that live-action role-playing when we get back?"

"I've been online with a few groups around the base back in Germany. They seem cool."

Tom's father, a career infantry sergeant, was happy when he joined the Army. He was the only parent from the platoon who was happy about his son's deployment to a war zone. Before his military service, Tom's dad barely noticed him—he had no interest in sports or physical activity other than dressing up to play cerebral games with other "losers."

"Good deal," Hero said. "Something to look forward to."

Slim and Carter hung back a few paces.
"So, you still going to jump ship after you finish your tour?" Carter asked.
"Once my paperwork is clear, I'm just going to drift into the

shadows, man. They'll buy me a ticket but I won't be on that plane," Slim said.

"What are you going to do?"

"I've got family that's already drifting around downtown."

"Right on."

"Need any drugs when we get back, you and Hero can just ask. Everyone else pays. I'm already working some business, so I can just get to it."

"I'll let you know. After all, the people who made this mess aren't on drugs, but they act worse than the people I know who are. Maybe that's a solution in itself," Carter said.

"Just peace, love and lot of drugs, man. That's what I'm in for after this mess. And of course, my inherited Gypsy skills."

"Of course," Carter said. He palmed the snack bars Slim had hid in his canteen case. "You've been practicing?"

"You wouldn't even know."

Carter unwrapped a bar and began to eat it, showing it off to Slim. He reached for one himself.

"Hey! Sonnofabitch!"

Carter laughed.

"Nice trick. I'll have to make sure I show you up now," Slim said. "Make sure you remember this when something goes missing."

"Check it out, Airborne shuffle at our six," Hero said.

"Looks like Ish," Carter said.

"Crappo. Everyone hold up. You know he knows we saw him. Drink water."

Sergeant Ish arrived huffing.

"Drink?" Hero asked.

"Thanks."

"I know you know, but this ain't like Baghdad, Sergeant. It's ten degrees hotter at least, plus dune-sand and the insane humidity. You'll get a fast ticket home running like that here."

"Room for one more in the crew?" he asked.

"Of course. Where'd we be without our beloved squad leader?" Hero asked.

"We've got a wager going on, would you like to join?" Carter asked.

"What's the wager?"

"Tell a story, to keep the long walk interesting. At the end everyone votes and the winner gets free eats at the canteen," Tom said.

"Yeah, why not."

"You can wait until last, that'd be after my turn, next, if you'd like some time to clear your head?"

Sergeant Ish upended Hero's canteen. He spat into the sand and wiped his lips on his arm. Carter offered his canteen to Hero in a no-look pass. Hero waived him off, hand-signed her thanks.

"All right then. Follow me and I'll get started with a story, called Failing St. George. It's from not too far in the future, near our long-lost duty station," Hero said.

9

Failing St. George

TWO GIANT trailers, nearly as wide as the narrow street itself, snarled traffic as a team of Turkish men in blue jumpsuits hastily unloaded boxes into our shared courtyard. Stoop-shouldered, ancient neighbors chided with glares and derogatory remarks in German. I narrowly averted laughing at them as wavering jowls and crepe paper faces created the type of caricatures that Norman Rockwell loved.

"Nice," Jen said. She stared after the nosy townsfolk, hands on her hips. "Maybe it was an allegorical dragon that the town's saint killed?"

"Hey, you wanted to move here. 'Oh, it's so great, lovely scenery. Quilted vineyards, gardens and orchards on the hills, forest pulls it all together,' remember?" I teased. The nippy air carried small flurries of snow into my disheveled brown hair. Long arms plunged deep into my pants pockets as I towered over the scurrying workmen as they tried to beat the creeping darkness.

"Oh, like you were any better. 'Did you see that the town's coat of arms is a dragon with a sword through its mouth?' It was all I could do to keep you from asking about the town's history rather than the house."

"At least I paid attention when he talked about the ancient foundations and tunnels."

"Is that supposed to help you?" she asked.

"Okay, we're both guilty. Time to pay the piper."

Our next-door neighbor ambled out of his house to complain as I supervised the installation of our small satellite dish.

"I'm going inside. Have fun," she said. The movers glanced at her as she bounded up the porch steps.

"We put television underground," he said. Herr Dampf's breath reeked of onions and vinegar.

"Yes, but not in English," I said in German. My hands stayed stuck in the pockets of my blue jeans. I glowered at Herr Dampf.

I do not know if it was a lack of further argument on his part, or if the shock that I understood their derision over the last few days that shut him up. He stomped back across the courtyard and slammed the door. For the rest of the morning, as men scuttled to and from the house with boxes, or heaved dressers up through the second story balcony, I caught glimpses of disgust through his veiled windows.

After lunch, the crew dug into the final layer of boxes. Jen came home early from work and unpacked inside the house. Our mounds of stuff filled each room to the brim.

"What's his deal?" she asked, passing paper cups of lemonade to the Turkish movers.

I explained the earlier conversation.

"What a Deutschebag," she said. "I thought something was

wrong—those hazel eyes of yours were full of fire. I was worried it was …" Jen nodded her head curtly to the side.

"Sorry, hon. It's nothing. Just a new born feud."

After the break, I helped unload the bookcases, and box after box of books. The trash from packaging was piled nearly as high as the courtyard gate. Two of the older men started to gather it up into tied bundles for the return run. Seizing the workers' distraction, our neighbor charged out of his front door.

We came nose-to-nose overtop a seat cushion. "You has too much things!" he declared.

I glanced at the old men binding cut up boxes near the gate. Their work knives glinted in the sunshine. They watched us with dark interest. "Bet you a round at the 'stube that they'll fit just fine," I said. Gently, I set the upholstery aside. "You don't look so good. Are you holding your breath?"

"You not the Boss," he said. "I am Boss." The fat little man looked about to burst. Veins in his face twitched under the scarlet and white of his emotionally strained complexion.

"You know, why don't we call the landlord to sort this out? You're obviously upset."

The fat little codger stood in his white cotton briefs and tanktop. He screamed, "Gunther not Boss. I am Boss!" He stuck his index finger into my chest and tapped like a pecking chicken.

I took a deep breath, exhaling my rage with it. Calm again I said, "First, I don't answer to you for anything. Second, if you poke me again, you will have to learn to write with your other hand."

The cretin stormed back into his adjacent house. He and his wife screamed for our benefit. They bemoaned the fate of the village, rambled on about the audacity and excess of Americans.

Without translation, it sounded like a couple professional wailers practiced in their entryway.

"You speak pretty good *Deutsche* for American," one of the Turks said.

His buddies openly laughed with the danger passed. The old men bound the last cardboard and trash, put their knives away. Practiced ease suggested previous careers more dangerous than household movers.

"Very Steven Segal," a younger one said. He sported a dusty black mohawk. He and another mover pantomimed the whole scene, with my character trouncing Herr Dampf.

I popped inside to fetch us all some beer.

"So, what you do?" the eldest asked. The Turk's squinted eyes appraised me like a fighter sizing up an opponent.

"I used to be a soldier. Now I'm a painter." Bubbles burst over the top of my bottle. The scent of the India Pale Ale reminded me of my employer, my actual job.

After sipping his own beer, the eldest said, "Nice town for that."

No one spoke afterwards.

A moment after we finished, their truck arrived. They slipped under the canvas canopy as dusk arrived. Some trick of the light darkened the street in shadow but missed their tan skin and coarse black hair.

"Everything in this place is timeless," I said as I watched the bodies melt into shadows under the tarpaulin as the well-abused carryall trundled down the alley. I stepped out to closed the doublewide gate, stepped in something wet.

"Dude." I cursed. "You ask for a sign …" Blood covered the bottom of my sneaker. I stepped lightly to the porch and set my shoes over the large rain gutter grate below to dry over night.

Failing St. George

I was washing dishes when the phone rang. Jen bounced into the room, this time with her uniform pants on and her naturally streaked blonde hair in a tight bun. "Hello?" she asked. "Yeah, okay. You sure? I'll let him know."

She zipped the front of her uniform blouse and I folded down her collar as we kissed good-bye. "Rob Dorian wants you to meet him at the 'visitor's bar' by the bus stop at noon."

"Thanks," I said while absently folding the towel.

"Said he already heard about the introductions?"

"Cool." I shrugged to dissuade further discussion. Between our jobs, neither could talk about work and we knew better than to ask. It would be nice to see Rob, and it made sense—two old soldiers getting together for a few beers because they lived nearby. Who knew painting could be so clandestine?

"See you tonight babe," Jen called from her car through the kitchen window. "Thanks for breakfast." Her Mini Cooper-S purred next to the porch.

"Just paying it forward. I'll get the gate."

"Say 'Hi' to Rob for me. It's nice having a friend to liaison," she said. She gunned the engine up the steep incline of mottled gray cobblestones. I heard the little car's turbo charger kick in down the block and smiled.

Around noon I walked down the street to the "visitor's pub," at least there I could have a couple Oktoberfest liters without feeling daggers plunge into my back. The sky was gray and white clouds clung to the hills topping the valley.

Walking into the bar's tent covered veranda, my eyes scanned for Rob. His text message said he'd reserved a corner table. He blended into the Oktoberfest garb in a heather-green hunting jacket and Tyrolean, replete with a trimmed grouse feather and a genuine dried Edelweiss safely pinned to his lapel.

"John, how are ya, old sod?" We shook hands as I sat down on the wooden bench opposite. While Germans normally have no regard for personal space, we still received a modicum of privacy. No one wanted to sit close to the potentially noisy, crass Americans. "Friendly," Rob shrugged in that subtle European way that meant everything and nothing at the same time.

"They grow on you."

"Like that stink you told me about? Creepy." A waitress whacked down two liter mugs of beer on the table, sloshing foam slightly. She looked like a medieval Goth, half out of her dress and did not give a wit. Rob dropped a ten-Euro note on her soaked tray and she vanished.

Blowing a divot into the head of mine, I took a deep, frothy gulp. "That's better."

"As Ben Franklin put it, 'Beer is proof that god loves us.'"

I took a deep breath. "Even this choking haze of cigarette smoke, beer and sweat is an improvement."

"That bad?" Rob tried to make contact with the waitress again, ordered a plate of Bavarian pretzels, sausages and pork patties with two beer refills for us.

"I shook the last whiff of sun-ripened-garbage-and-flower essence from my nostrils just before I got here. I clean more often, even using straight bleach, but it doesn't go away for more than a day or two. And it's not just one part of the house, it drifts man. Now I'm smelling it around town in little pockets as I walk down the street …"

"Noises too, still?" Rob was jovial until you got to his eyes.

Failing St. George

There, hard analysis lived. Focused hazel irises pierced to the heart of whatever matter lay before them. "How's the painting coming? Is this town giving your muse more to work with?"

We could not talk directly, dodging business like swordsmen in battle we ran down our surveillance and instructions through the noise of the singing Germans, sloshing mugs, and polka music.

"It goes. I'm getting a much more vibrant scheme to work with here, and there are a lot of options when it comes to perspective and shading. I love these hamlets—so developed and rich. The earth just comes through so much more clearly than in the cities ... a more equal footing of nature and development, coming up through the cracks. People here fit into the landscape in the same way, like they're carved from the earth too."

"Sounds like a rich environment for work. I'm sure that the people in the cities would love some of that in their houses."

"Glimpses, for fun ... a safe distance, maybe," I said. "And you? What's new?"

Rob Dorian's cover was a visiting climate scientist, on loan to the European Space Agency from the United States' Jet Propulsion Laboratory. "Just keeping an eye on things—same old, same old. I'm tracking more climate variations in the area, but of course the higher-ups don't believe it. Doesn't fit the party line."

"Whether we want to believe it or not, climate change is here," I said.

"And with it, what comes next, eh?"

"A different rabbit hole?" We both chuckled in that way that soldiers do while contemplating their imminent bloody deaths.

Another liter of beer down and the waitress dropped two more big mugs on our sopping blue and white checkered tablecloth. I smiled in that fine continental tradition that kindly invited the recipient to drop dead at their earliest convenience. It was expected.

"So," Rob sipped his dark beer through the foam, "How about that hot blonde sugar mama you got payin' your bills? How's Jen doing?"

"Fine, fine. You'd know better, but after hours she's adjusted well. That wrinkled old codger gave us a headache at first, but other than the evil eye he's been keeping to himself. They both have."

"And you?" He diverted his eyes to the depths of his mug.

"Keeping the post-army weight off, but not having a PT schedule means that this is about as much weight lifting as I've been getting."

"You could stand to keep up your cardio …" he peeked over the rim. "You know?" My heart rate sped up a little—*Did I miss something important in our exchange? Was Rob trying to remind me of a veiled warning?*

It was my turn to shrug. Rob lifted his hat enough to run fingers through his salt and pepper hair. He looked like Cary Grant or Jimmy Stewart framed by a Hitchcock lens. Just like in those noir movies, I was not quite sure where the darkness laid and what it meant.

The food finished and the beer bubbling through my blood, it was time for us to slip from this tangent back into our respective positions. As I walked outside, I buttoned up my peacoat. Rob's bus roared away from the stop, apparently playing 'Chicken' with the rest of traffic. Compared to the dank fetor that crept through the house every few days, the wind that drew through the hamlet smelled of the forest that lay beyond the meadows and orchards climbing the walls of our village. It hung heavy with the threat of a cold rain.

A few weeks passed and I carted off enough canvas to look like a respectable professional. People in Wiesbaden and Heidelberg bought the paitings and made a bit of a fuss about it. The Wiesbadener Kurier newspaper wanted to do an interview for their Sunday edition and preferred to visit in the studio. I explained that I worked outside, but that we could meet over coffee at our house and I'd have an old friend interpret for me.

"So," Rob said. "You weren't kidding--does it always smell like sewer here?"

"I invite you to visit and you deride my quaint village? What smell?" I poured some coffee once the pot stopped gurgling and passed him a mug.

He gratefully gulped down a mouthful. I unconsciously stared, knowing how hot the brew was. "Right. How's things with the neighbors? Still feuding?"

"It's all right. We just leave each other alone, pretend the other doesn't exist. It's funny how hard we actually work to avoid each other."

"You know, it almost smells like Baghdad," Rob said.

"Not quite. It's missing that top note."

"I guess they haven't burned any bodies for a while?"

"Never mistake that smell." I poured two schnapps into the mugs. We both quieted down.

"Seriously, I can talk to the public affairs office about this if you want. We can get Jen a transfer, if you think it's going to interfere. She's a security office for the ambassador's whole staff. It's not like it'd look out of the ordinary."

"Thanks bro, I appreciate it. Not necessary. They're just some old biddies." I slurped down my liquor. "They've run out of life before living."

The news van peeked over the top of the wall by the gate.

Jen arrived early from work, passing the news crew as they drove out of the tiny, sloped cobblestone courtyard.

"How did the interview go? Do you want to go up to the Goethe monument after dinner? I brought home some takeout from a dönner kebap stand down the street. Got some salads and such," she said. Her gym bag hit the floor with a heavy thud.

"Went fine. Sounds great. Rob says 'Hi' back."

"You boys have fun? Didn't drink too much, did you?" Jen asked as she unpacked the cartons. The smell of grilled meat, flatbread and spicy sauces wafted from the kitchen bar as I sorted her fresh laundry.

"We did. A walk sounds nice and romantic," I said. "I'll show you the scorch marks on the north village gate ruins. There've been a lot of fires over the centuries. Not just our house, but the whole town's just built on top of the rubble."

She never bothered to look up. "Sounds fascinating," she said. A plate slid across the bar to me. The television blared to life while we ate. Soon we were out the door and heading up the valley towards the nature trailhead at the old north gate. Jen pressed on without hesitation towards the monument.

"You know," she panted, "You could hide anything in this bramble." Unruly hedges of blackberry briar lined the narrow vineyard paths, so thick that light barely penetrated their prickly depths.

Every step felt like my blood turned to acid in my legs as we climbed. The burn made me rethink the climb up to the monument. *Not exactly romantic to get all cozy when you're panting and smell like a sweaty goat,* I thought. The wind picked up. It found the slightest gaps between the togs on my jacket. Jen put her knit cap back on. Out of breath, we reached Goethe's monument. "Well?"

"I can't see it," she said. She searched the rooftops for our television dish.

"It's been a couple months. Maybe more people have got them now, keeping up with the Joneses."

"Yeah, since we moved in. The house is barely together. Where's the water bottle?"

"For that matter, where is the house?" I turned around, looked down on the village. "It looks charming at a distance. Maybe the consulate will move us again?"

Jen chuckled as we strolled along an alley filled with ancient retaining walls and purple climbing flowers. The occasional passersby from town ignored us.

"Funny," she said. "I don't think a bitchy old fart or two constitutes a terrorist threat or hot spot."

"Maybe you were right about the dragon," I said. "I've taken a closer look at the other versions around town. He's usually got a spear, inflicting a mortal wound to the beast. This sword just had the thing pinned through the bottom jaw or something."

"I think you're still pissed about Mr. Deutschebag and are itching for a fight, civilly, through the town's artwork."

"Maybe I should paint a mural of Siegfried at the Drachenfelds, or George in full attack, then hang it from the balcony so people see it over the gate."

"Try not to piss off the whole town, babe. They might put you in stocks," she said.

"What, under the thousand-year-old linden tree?" The sky darkened as clouds gathered as they crossed the hills. We started the downward slope, back towards home.

"Heard they used to hang folks there," Jen said.

"I read that it was where they had the people's court, but no one was executed," I said. "The library's antique documents collection listed several settlement hearings between the occupants of our house and the neighbors since the Dark Ages. Evidently living in our house has always been trouble."

"So that's why the blood trails keep showing up. We're cursed—like the story of the two local kids who snuck off to play Romeo and Juliet back in the day. Either way, that's probably where you'll end up," she said. "I'll just drive home one night and see you clapped up in the church courtyard or something." We laughed together.

"I'll try to be nicer," I said.

We walked back down the hillside, hand in hand. After showers at home, I made a couple Tanqueray and tonics. Mindless television soothed our spent effort while we remedied the missed romance of the nature walk. The bed was cool and soft as we slipped in.

Several crashes hit with creaks and moans in the night. Animal sounds—like feral cats squared off against wild dogs—quickly faded as I woke up. My eyes opened, sought shapes in the dimness. I could not figure out where the sounds came from, or their cause. It sounded as if someone took quick, light steps on the roof, then knocked boxes against the side of the house's upper floor.

"What was that?!" Jen turned on the lamp by the bed.

"Probably the cats."

Failing St. George

"Go check, wouldya?"

Odd creaks, thumps and crashes had struck at odd hours inside the house off and on since we moved in. Usually they were not loud enough to wake Jen up. I stretched, then slid out from under the comforter. I walked the upstairs and downstairs rooms before coming back to bed. "Nothing," I said. "Twelve restaurants in this cramped neighborhood. Chalk it up to one of the other houses."

I rolled over, felt her unease. I said, "Living so close together it's possible their noise created some strange echoes on our end." It was the same logic I used to explain that vagrant fetor, even the occasional blood smears on the morning pavement.

Weeks turned into months. My paintings were picked up in Wiesbaden by local galleries. They sold in an idle trickle, as people wanted everything American, while they lambasted U.S. politics and our national identity in the streets. We hardly left the house and shunned the locals in turn.

"You must be pretty stoked," Jen said. She sat her valise by the shoe rack at the front door. "Even people in Frankfurt are talking about your work."

"It's totally killer. Try this." I stepped out of the kitchen, handed her a spoon of sauce.

She smacked her lips. "Delicious."

Over dinner, we chatted about the office intrigues and news from back in the states.

"So, I was going over the town histories again when I found a bunch of records from when they rebuilt the tower. There was a lot of construction after the Second World War. Some of the permits included our house and the ones adjacent. They listed the resident and owner as Heinrich Dampf."

Jen was befuddled. "No."

"Yes."

"It's probably a family name or something."

"I know, I mean, he's old but not old enough to have been a home owner in the forties."

"Wow."

"Even more—they've owned these properties for hundreds of years. Remember that fire in the fifteen hundreds I told you about? The Dampfs were there too. Barely escaped." Between the last forkfuls of dessert I said, "Tunnels. Used to be between here and the ruins' court."

"Crazy," she said. Jen cleared the dishes.

Over the winter, every so often, I ran into our neighbor in the courtyard. He ignored me, drove his decrepit Opel Vectra or shambled between his basement workshop below the house and garage. It was some sort of vestigial out building down the hillside from before the fire, I reconed. He took armloads of lumpy, nondescript bags in, but I never saw them come out. I was more interested in what lengths he went to avoid eye contact as he scurried around, than suspicious of what was going on in there. The antics held my interest more than the American television he was so upset over.

It was a Thursday in March when Jen came through the front door with six yellow bags of recyclable trash. She huffed.

I said, "Is the budget so bad that they're making you take out the garbage now too?"

"Funny. No, I found these just inside of our neighbor's garage."

"What the hell?" I had enough. "He used to be funny in a geriatric way, but this is wrong—dangerous. Wait, what were you doing in his garage?"

"They propped open its gate, just outside of it. I saw the English labels through the plastic, then saw that it was stuff like mac-and-cheese, tortillas ... our stuff," she said. Her anger was about to boil over onto me.

"That's like three months' worth. Man, we share all our bins. He could be stealing identity information or worse," I said. "I'm on it. Just let me take care of it in the morning so I don't punch his lights out?"

"Please don't make it worse than it is," Jen said. "I'll talk to security at work, call the credit bureaus, check our accounts and stuff while you straighten him out. Find out if he's killing rats or whatever, while you're at it."

The next morning, I woke up ready to fight. I stalked across our shared courtyard, trash in hand. I was livid. I rang the neighbor's bell, pounded his door till it groaned and creaked, then tapped relentlessly on every pane of glass I could reach.

No answer.

I heard a timber creak.

Workshop.

"Herr Dampf?" I asked.

Yellow bags in tow and courage thundering in my veins, I unlatched the doublewide wooden doors. Carefully I walked down the coarsely made steps into the basement. Odd loft spaces gaped above me. Doors doubled back in obscure directions. Everything sat in shadows under the single, bare electric light bulb.

Basement? I thought. *Catacombs.*

I looked down one of the eldritch passages.

Before I could investigate, I heard more noise down a different corridor. It came from behind another set of double-doors. This time it sounded like conversation. I could not make out the words, but the language was closer to Irish than German in its strange vowel pairings and gutturals. These doors were rough-shod covers over a metal cage. The arched threshold was made of rough-hewn sandstone bricks. A large metal crossbar lay against the wall. Apparently it held the door shut from the outside.

The door opened with a groan, the damp musty smell of the basement took on a more sinister top note. Rob was right.

Death.

I dropped my bags, and turned to close the gate and set the crossbar against who or whatever crept down there. I thought to call the police when I heard a skittering sound behind me. I spun around. A heavy clap resounded in my skull, my knees buckled.

The lights went out.

"Oh, so nice to join us, our dear neighbor," Herr Dampf said. He sat cross-legged before me. A peat fire burned low in the dimness. Shafts of light pooled from holes high above. "We was wanting to introduce you and your wife properly, but her schedule ..." He shrugged, chuckled to himself.

The cavern was dim and musty. Pockets of gas belched across the semi-fluid terrain of the gigantic cave. An enormous, raised parade deck of cut pink stone glittered in the weak incandescent light from drainage grates above. A copper funnel system that mimicked industrial liquor stills ran along the roof, with baffles

Failing St. George

around the drains. Tiny quartz crystals ran through the stone and gave it a natural polished shine. Four-dozen Turks walked a perimeter in planked shoes, cicled inwards towards some amorphous goal. The men held long poles, like ferrymen or gondoliers in Venice. They jabbed them deep into the ground as they tentatively walked on its sodden surface. The ground shifted and swelled below them, as if their efforts pried some sinister evil from the forgotten depths. Villagers stood twenty across and five deep on the stone floor and peoppered alcoves in red and white robes. The ostentatious devils observed the arcane ritual and let their thrall carry the dirty work.

Ground? I analyzed in my disjointed state. *Bog.*

"You came on your garbage?" the neighbor asked.

"And you've got 'shrooms?" *Concussion,* I thought. *And bad jokes.*

Laughing, he said, "No, no sir. Something from a different type of secret. We telled the children, even Gunther, about Siegfried. How his dragons didn't all die. How their blood can extend life. Over a longer time, through the wars, stories came legends, finally dissolved into local *eventyr*—empty threats."

"What's in the bog?" I asked. I winced and spat bile onto the ancient cobblestone. It felt like my old boxing partner had beaten me into the canvas again.

"The Nassaus," he said. "Everyone thinks they were to watching our five errant knights. It was their king's interest in the thing that kept them on the hill. Far up the hill."

I could not keep up with him. Barely breathing, my eyesight dimmed and came back, over and over, like a television tube on the fritz. Ringing filled my ears to the same effect. I reached for the back of my head, chains jingled. My turn to sigh.

"You see," he said, "we have a unique recycling program here, you may say, first of its kind and no stopping for more than thirty-five generations. Five families bent it to its purpose—invaders, trash, whatever. Takes everything, makes gas out for the heating, we don't have to die ... incredible eater. But you become familiar with it soon enough.

Do you wonder, how with all these restaurants we could manage the waste? How many drunks ever hassled you in town—waken you in middle of the night? Eh? Or rodent?"

The plank-walkers stirred, plunged their staves deep into the bog in a faster, concentrated effort. The peaty earth heaved and swelled. My body mimicked the landscape, vomiting again. Imagined arms reached up from the pit of my gut, clawing for the surface. I tried to aim for my neighbor.

"Excuse me sir, but he's with me," Rob said. He came from behind Herr Dampf. I was disoriented, transfixed by the village people's scene. I heard a heavy bolt slam a round into a wicked sounding weapon. Rob packed heat like a battleship.

Jen screamed. "John!"

Shots rang out in three quick pairs. Blood and heavier wetness flew in pieces from Heinrich Dampf. Rob came to my side, cut me loose with bolt cutters. Jen slid a new magazine into her Browning, threw the slide home. Her left hand ruffled my hair, then was back in place in a two-hand pistol grip. She scanned the crowd of liveried locals and staff-wielding Turks as their attention shifted towards us.

"Can you move?" he asked. "I didn't buy that they were just old biddies." Rob stood over the corpse like it was just so much garbage. Jennifer's Browning Hi-Power pistol fired into the crowd as they reached the cobblestone shore. I threw an arm over each

Failing St. George

of their shoulders and we scaled the stairs, pausing to cover our escape with hollow points.

Bodies dropped as Rob turned our defense into offense, but the townsfolk stayed in their reveries. A few Turks ran headlong toward adjacent stairwells and us. "They'll be trying to flank us," Rob said.

The bog exploded as something massive broke through the surface's crust. An unearthly call blared throughout the cavern—no doubt it resounded in the town above as their creature, whatever it was—is, emerged from its dank grave.

Thin tentacles, impossibly long, first broke the surface. They reached up to the roof of the underground bog. Like a squid's, shorter, stout appendages rose to pull the head of the beast through the bog's peaty crust. A giant yellow and black eye stared at us sidelong, its match lost across the face, hooded by the upturned forward edge of its carapace. It body was an oily slick, streaked with falling clumps of rotted matter and some unknown dark maroon substance. From the way debris chaffed off, a hard shell encased the thing rather than skin. The distal edge of the huge carapace flipped half a dozen Turks off their feet as it shoveled peat in an oddly fluid wave into the air. The thing's call was deafening, now that it was above the surface. Huge forelimbs, an exaggerated form of a pachyderm's, struck forward onto the stone landing as the creature raised half its bulk from the depths.

The creature belched gas from its nostrils, three teams of men with flamethrowers and halberds took defensive positions on the edge of the stone deck. They launched a single, coordinated burst and the roof of the cavern burst into flames, quickly blown out through the surface grills and extinguished. The dragon flailed, thin tendrils lassoed five of the nine defenders.

Jennifer fired, saving the men their bloody fate as their corpses found their way into the omnivorous maw of the dragon. The slide of her Browning Hi-Power locked back with a sudden click. "I'm out," she said. Her face lost all composure, Jen stood still and silent. Rob unloaded a stream of flaming-hot jacketed shells towards the dragon.

Replacements streamed out from alcoves along the mammoth stone floor. The beast exhaled a noxious torrent thick enough to dim the surface light and turn the air into a swirling haze. The previously reverent villagers collapsed in the miasma or held their breath to run for fresh air. More fell prey to the beast, eaten alive or drowned under the peaty depths. As Rob's weapon continued to churn the air, pockets of flame exploded as the rounds ignited the creature's ether.

"Go." Rob shouted. "I'll be right behind you. Go!" he said. "Flamethrowers, the gas …" We ran ahead, no time for questions.

"How do you know the way?" I asked.

"Floor dust is scattered. It's the way we came down." She trotted with her pistol fixed ahead of her. I knew it was empty, so did she. We ran faster for it.

The catacombs turned and I saw the inside of our neighbor's basement garage. The air in the tunnel was hard to breath—it hissed. I yelled, "Move!"

The rocks overhead gave way and collapsed the tunnel right behind us. I still felt the heat from the natural gas fed fire behind the debris. We booked through the old gate into his underground antechamber, and I saw Jen violently swing her pistol butt around the side of the door. I rushed out and German police wrestled us down in a dog pile. Jen said nothing as they slaped handcuffs on his and took blood samples.

Failing St. George

Soon we emerged from the basement into the courtyard under the guard of the Polizei. Flashing lights lit up the village in blue, red and orange. A few sirens wailed and chaos reigned. I smelled smoke. Fire trucks' hoses cranked up the humidity as they soaked buildings around several structure fires in town. Avoiding capture, somehow Rob came around behind the glut of German cops. Through his assertive sphere of influence he managed to take control of 'the prisoners,' with a gender mixed pair of police escorts.

Apparently cursing in Iraqi Arabic at the Gordian knot of traffic twisted through the town, Rob passed intelligence under the noses of our escorts. "I'm taking you to the police station, but it is only until the embassy's people show up. They're being extremely hush-hush, no idea who they're sending or where they're from."

Rob swerved around an ambulance hell-bent on being first to somewhere. "Their specialist will be there shortly. Even for embassy guys, they're being ultra secretive. A cleaning crew has been sent in to the catacombs posing as ESWE Gas workers. They'll liquidate the creature if necessary. Mission accomplished, John."

I tried to make eye contact with Jen, she avoided it. The cops took us down to the city, where we were booked. We were reunited in an interrogation room, lit by an off-hue fluorescent light bar that flickered. Years of stale cigarette smoke pumped in from the ventilation duct.

After half an hour of no conversation, two police—a cop and a detective from their looks—barged in. They focused their attention on her.

"What happened?" the detective asked.

"Start from when you arrived," the cop said. I avoided pointing out that we were separated at the time. Jen stayed mum too.

"...Rob saw what happened from the bar across the street. He approached me as I pulled into the courtyard. He was obviously distraught, at the time I thought he was distraught. Now I would say he was terrified. He visibly shook, mashing his hands together," Jen said.

"...And when did you see him last? ..."

"...Rob fell behind to ensure our escape, rambling ... unintelligible," Jennifer said.

"...And he didn't object to you ventilating your neighbor? ..."

I wiped my lips, a sodden paper bag dangled between my hands. I said, "—in German, English and that Celtic sounding language."

She shifted in her draped wool blanket under cobweb streaked wet hair. Jen piped up, "Fortunately, they reached a critical mass just in time. They saw us as a nuisance and wanted to clean up—evidently like they had for quite a while. Go down there. You'll see what we're talking about. The cavern was a huge ruin, all built on top of and paved over. Centuries they've been hiding that thing, whatever it was—is, for—dammit."

She pounded the table, shouted at the German police. "Whether you believe us or not, we demand to contact the U.S. Embassy. I have certain diplomatic rights."

The German cop sat across from us. His shadowed eyes belied disbelief over our written statements. The white paper's horrific ink scribbles stood out against the backdrop of the cop's tan and green uniform. He said, "We will release you to them when your blood tests come back, if they are negative. As for your friend, Mr.

Failing St. George

Dorian, he also has … certain diplomatic immunities." Suspicion dripped from every word.

"Neither of you have been taking intoxicants, no pills or maybe some recreational—" The officer's plain-clothes partner fixed me with a melodramatic, sympathetic look.

I gathered all the sanity and force I could muster, glared straight into his eyes. "No."

"Madam, your hands test positive for gunpowder residue. Your weapon was fired recently," the uniform said. He still clutched the file.

"Part of my duties at the embassy are to provide security, I am licensed for concealed carry here. According to the accords between our countries I am also permitted to self-defense with deadly force."

"You both look and smell like a sewer," the detective said.

"Sir, you have a very nasty bump on your head," the cop said. "What you are saying sounds like a … *traum*—hallucination."

"Perhaps you drank from the wrong glass while painting?"

"What sounds equally as implausible however, are the stories of your neighbors." The policeman shuffled the sheaf. "Mister Dampf—is nowhere to be found. Several people in the community say you shot at them, killed others. We have no bullets, though your weapon was still hot when the squad picked you up. We have no bodies."

The detective leered at us. "The basement door you spoke of leads into a very old but collapsed tunnel." He slammed both palms on the table.

"Sounds like you're digging," I said.

A voice behind us said, "Your claims are fantastic." A man in a noticeably neater suit stepped from artfully covered shadows. "Almost beyond belief."

"Almost," Jennifer said.

"Gentlemen, you are excused." The man came forward. His pomaded hair glowed in the fluorescent light. A perfect line of moustache shadowed his lip, counterpoint to his tailored suit and tie, drew your eyes to his mouth. Neat white teeth flashed, added to the shine of his oiled skin, with rimless pince-nez to add authority to his suave. He sat across from us as the two policemen quietly, briskly left the interrogation room.

"…almost …" she echoed.

"Almost, my dear—Andrew Durst," he said. "I'm a liaison from the State Department. We work on cases like yours, quite a unique position." He deftly gathered all the police notes and evidence into a sealed bag that incinerated itself like flash paper as he sent it spinning across the room like a frisbee. Jen had her game face on. "All those children's stories came from somewhere you know. Just be glad it wasn't what became of *Der Struwwelpeter* or the hell that was politely turned from *Hänsel und Gretel*."

Rob walked in. Jen was not surprised, which surprised me. The whole time I tried to comfort her, let her know … *Did she speak Iraqi?* Somehow she was tipped off. "What's going on Dorian? You told her and not me?" I asked. I sought out his eyes, but he avoided me too.

"Thanks," he said to Jen. "You really made me sound like the drunken lunatic I asked for." He slid into the shadows without meeting my eyes.

"I'll be taking over for our friend Rob, as your special liaison from here out. Now, in order to move you … We need to

Failing St. George

have you sign some papers. Not this police rubbish—secrets. You understand?"

Jen said, "What about the people? What about that ... whatever it is? What—"

"—All in due time, ma'am. You should know that there are things you cannot, are not allowed to know."

"But monsters? Psychotic villagers? And Rob? Maybe I'm high, maybe Nessie and Babe the Blue Ox are just wandering about too," she said.

I reached out to comfort her. She shoved me away, drew her hand up to slap me. It dropped in total frustration.

"Sir, they are all being dealt with as we sit here. Have no fear, we're here to help," Andrew said. He turned a smile so polished it moved your emtions before it registered in your eyes. "Of course, now that you've seen what lurks beneath, maybe you would like to join your husband and his friend in our attempts to keep it there?"

"You've got to be kidding me."

"You know how there was that thing in the desert I couldn't tell you about?" She just stared at me. "Remember 1001 Arabian Nights? Aladdin? It doesn't really have a lot of musical duets."

"Just a few screams," Rob said.

"I literally fell into this world," I said. I reached for her hands and she pulled away again, slower. "How do you tell your love that you've kept them in harm's way without their knowledge for years? That while they've been tending your wounds, you've been faking the real causes?"

Andrew stood close enough that the dangling lamp in the otherwise dim interrogation room only lit his face from the bridge down, focusing our eyes on his lips. "We are the Huntsman who sets upon the big, bad wolf. The Tin Man and the Lion who defend Dorothy, what comes after the things that go bump in the night."

"Lies, all this time?" Jen turned her head to Andrew as he hovered between us. "Platitudes and nice speeches won't cut it with me, Jack."

"Maybe this will. John fell into this sand trap, but you charged in." He laid down a business card. On it a pale blue globe and crossed olive branches on a white linen card. Below the crest was a phone number. Above the crest the initials I.P.A.—Investigators of Preternatural Affairs, United Nations—and the Latin motto, *Per Obscurum, in Luminarium.* Through the Darkness, into the Light. "We like your style."

10

Leadership

"SOUNDS like that albino monitor lizard we found at the weigh point," Ish said.

"Yeah, if it had mated with a camel spider and it's offspring were exposed to gamma radiation," Tom said.

"Push," Ish said.

"It's a great day to be a soldier!" Tom exclaimed, his hands sunk deep into the sand.

"Gamma rays destroy living tissue, dude. That's why Bruce Banner had to have special genetics—otherwise he'd just be a piece of Sergeant Ish's barbeque." Hero skipped the order and dropped to start doing pushups. Carter and Slim were down before her first repetition finished.

Faced with a Pyrrhic victory, Sergeant Ish said, "Recover. Drink water."

Tom was visibly dehydrated. Hero waived off Carter's canteen again, signaled to give it to the Private instead.

"Can we take a knee, Sergeant?"

"All right."

Slim helped Tom from falling over into the sand without

exposing the kindness to the Sergeant. Hero locked eyes on Tom's, searched for any signs that might betray heat exhaustion.

"Come on, let's go, ladies," Ish said. "I've got a story to tell."

From the ether, Slim produced a bandana, soaked it in water and handed it to Tom. Out of the corner of her eye, Hero tracked silent messages from Carter, Slim and Tom. The Private recovered and gave a thumbs-up to Hero. Ish led the group.

"Now if you're done, I'll start my own. 'Our Last Stand.'"

11

Our Last Stand

THE AIR was thick. Dust clogged noses and engine manifolds alike, while the reek of unwashed bodies tainted every taste. We pushed relentlessly through the desert. Shield formations scuttled around us. Earthmovers plowed aside obstacles. We pressed on, with blistered feet and burning lungs. Stretched across the African Sahel zone, our divisions were the last organized wave of humanity to repel the invaders. Behind it all was the faint, malignant odor of death.

Inescapable. My thoughts were my own, but I kept my mouth shut. *Monsters and their nasty little pets. What the hell is the point? It's only a matter of time before we're just so much cooked food for these guys.*

A public relations officer walked backwards in front of me, capturing video that could be used to fill in news, print and propaganda around the globe. He had to hock a war that was an easy sell—fight or be exterminated. Why not use a young black Non-Com? We were marching across Africa after all. Besides at six-foot two-inches and a lean 240 pounds, I looked straight out of comic book.

"So, Sergeant John Tyler, you've been in the desert fighting the aliens for nearly a year?"

"A few months shy, but sure," I said.

"You and your men must be tired, though it looks like you've received support from all the nations. Is there anyone back home or elsewhere you'd like to thank?"

"The U.N. has been great to us, care packages from strangers have really kept us on the ball, while we're here." This was the standard party line in our briefings—include everyone, don't ask but insinuate more is needed.

His spiel was slick as axle grease. "Those lizards are everywhere and their masters are incredible, building-size. What seems to work best?" he asked.

"We call 'em Jellies around here. They look like those old 1950's gelatin molds. As such, microwave cannons work great, but it's a suicide job getting close enough …"

The P.R. officer coughed.

As we marched on I continued, filling in the soldier speak for softer audiences. "Though they work great on the boulders they throw down on us. Thank goodness for all the world's pilots—they can get close enough to hit the Je … Masters, since firing ballistic missiles are like pop-flies to the big guys."

Satisfied with a few usable bites, the PRO fell back to some trailer to do his work. I was still hoping he'd trip on a corpse's arm or foot on the way back. Despite the Shield-bearers' and Engineers' efforts to clear away the dead, every few yards body parts poked up through the sand. Grisly reminders of what we fought.

"Listen up," I roared. "They think we're beat. Easy pickin's for their 'little friends.' Like the Op says, let's show 'em what Humans do and kick their jellied asses."

Our Last Stand

The troops raised a thunder that echoed across the dunes. Months of fighting wore them down physically, but their spirits were in good shape. Fighting for their lives and the right to exist galvanized them beyond civilized tolerances for aches and scrapes. Less than a year passed since an apparent meteor storm covered the world's equatorial zones in extraterrestrial bubbles, which grew to towering globs of alien sentience. Academic curiosity quickly turned to ghastly news, as millions of humans and untold numbers of wildlife became raw genetic material. They were used both for the Jellies themselves and facsimilated creatures from Earth's age of dinosaurs. As human armies tried to regain territory, the aliens used their membranes to launch giant stones like blasts from a shotgun.

Platoon's down to twenty. Only Grace and Quinones are left from the original landing. How long will Operation Human Resolve *hold? Those 'troopers better make the LZ.*

The boulders that the Jellies launched came skittering down in a rain of pebbles now, thanks to our microwave cannons. Concussion waves built up dunes as we sat in position, pinned down by the fire control computers' ability to track so many targets. As the Artillery dispersed the incoming boulders, they left the Engineers and Shield-bearers to protect us from stone rain. The hot little rocks particularly annoyed soldiers in mechanical suits like Quinones.

He was a heavy-set Puerto Rican, but he could move like Thor's Hammer in his rig. With all of their firepower and the exoskeleton, they had a harder time ducking under shields with their bulk. It resulted in the operators developing skin that looked like the surface of the moon. The clamor of pebbles on metal-ceramic shields drowned out the din of battle. Between bombardments, we ran up the dunes into hell.

"—ck Cousin It!" Private Quinones said under another rain of rocks.

"We're moving on the next break," I said.

Grace nodded. "Okay boss." Her thin frame moved like a stalking cat—quick, focused on every detail. Light blonde hair, blue eyes, and an expressive face, Grace was a model in the days before the Reserves and National Guard were depleted. Then the Jellies literally absorbed San Francisco coming up from Central America, obliterating her life. Now she had to do something else. Revenge had a certain appeal.

White phosphorous burned brilliant, exploding in a stream outside of the trench. After days of fighting side by side, the shield crews moved with the same precision as my own troops.

"Quinones, make good use of that fire. Light 'em up."

Grace shouted, "Support barrage on its way, boss!"

Before this desperate war threw us together, we would never have met. No way would you find Grace or Q coming to an immigrant law charity. I couldn't imagine life without them now. They were extensions of myself. So were the others we lost over the hump from Lagos. How funny that my life is now dedicated to burning illegal immigrants alive. *It's strange what you can get used to.* Of course, we never took cases for human felons back in the day either.

Ten-gauge automatic shotguns ripped apart the raptor-sized creatures while close-quarters flak cannons unloaded on their larger cousins. We climbed over shockwave dunes as the sand was pummeled to dust. Animal screams told us the effect of our cannon fire.

"Too far. Hold and defend," I said.

Our Last Stand

The field commanders realized early on that guns run out of bullets and men can only carry so many high explosives. As everything old becomes new again, the powers that be gave us new high-tech machetes for what the Joe's started calling "the Romero Option."

Rifles dropped to their slings as creatures got close to our defenses. Only Quinones with his higher position in the suit was allowed to continue blasting away.

"Bayonets. Cut 'em down!"

The platoon formed a horseshoe to do battle against the onslaught. Every soldier left was an expert marksman and swordsman by default. Survival demanded it. We fought three men deep, hacking the enemy to pieces. They were little more than animals. The opportunity for fresh meat witout a fight distracted them from us.

As the 'saurs cannibalized their dismembered, our Shieldbearers moved forward to deflect the creatures. Engineers bulldozed behind us in massive armored columns.

"That was close," Grace said as she checked for wounded and counted ammunition.

"We're getting tired. It shows," I said.

"At least we made it through another hop."

"When Becky's side started to break, that one 'saur—"

"But we caught it. Once they had each other to eat they weren't so interested in us," she said and laughed.

"I know," I sighed.

Tanks and paladins fired overhead, worrying at the enormous amoeba-like invaders far in the distance. Close air support thundered overhead. I thought of the Brits dropping in on their landing zone. We were still at least five good hops away.

"Listen up. We've got to get to that LZ. Those troopers are counting on us. We are not going to let them turn into piñatas for some bigger lizards. That artillery is going to cut things down into smaller bites we can handle. We can't let the fire die down this time. Move."

The next couple of jumps, the 'saurs were so torn up by artillery we just had to keep moving. In the time that I could, my body moved into self-preservation mode. I walked, talked and stayed alert yet I was little more than a zombie. I didn't react when the stony hail pelted us through the gaps in the shields. Even when fist-sized rocks pounded the earth, I just kept shuffling.

After fighting for two weeks pushing the alien Sluagh against the eastern shelf, I drifted in the seeming endless stream of memories. I blocked out the battles and deaths of loved ones as they clamored to be heard.

I returned to the last chance I had to relax—the United Nations base in Lagos. "They are not dinosaurs. They are not dragons. Honestly, the scientists are still trying to agree on just what they are. But, all you need to know for your job is that they are nasty, smart, carnivorous devils. Their brains are small, they're mostly meat. Sever the tendons … here and here," the intelligence briefer fanned the crowd with his shaking pant legs. "They will fall. Immobilized they will still be a threat, but no longer capable of moving."

"So how did Barney get here?" one incredulous Captain asked.

The nervous Lieutenant tried to stem the tide of comments. "In ships. They traveled at 3G's, and we are able to employ the Newtonian field against them even though it was designed to cover terrestrial targets."

Who cares? I thought. *I need some chow and a shower before we kit up, you sod. Maybe I can get a draught from one of the Irish guys, better yet, one of the Irish girls ...*

"I understand that there are more ships coming from above the disk?"

A female CERN scientist broke in to help the struggling Lieutenant. "We still don't know that, sir, but modeling indicates some sort of gravitational attraction was used to arc their trajectory over the galactic disk. It exceeds our understanding of both propulsion and gravity."

The crowd of UN troop commanders settled down under the weight of her authority. She moved from the wings of the stage towards the Lieutenant, a vanguard of support.

An Indian officer asked, "What about the big jellies themselves?"

"Are we still calling them that?" a public relations officer said.

A female dissident rebuked her for politicizing their genocidal enemies. "'saurs and Jellies," she said.

"We have no political dialogue with the enemy," the Lieutenant said. "Close air support, naval gunnery, artillery and low-yield nukes seem to get the job done ... eventually. We have used new weapons systems to match their physical strength. Pneumatic armor, microwave cannons ... We have also revived some very old techniques with modernized Shield-bearers and battle engines."

"So we'll be fighting in radiation?" a German officer asked.

"NBC suits?" an anonymous voice said. "There's no where near enough, let alone decon supplies. There'll be nowhere for us to go. Even in suits it's just prolonging the inevitable."

The crowd's exasperated grumblings grew to threaten the

speaker system carrying the Lieutenant's brief across the prefabricated lecture hall. He struggled to dominate them over the noise.

"Casualty projections are at 85 percent. This war is not for ideologies or for territory. We are fighting for the Earth itself, for our species to survive. The human population has already been whittled down to an estimated three and a half billion.

You and your troops have all registered your genetic material at the collection points. You are guaranteed prominent lineages in repopulation efforts, regardless of your individual survival. Should you make it through the battle …"

The outcry was an incessant rumble. The Lieutenant was visibly afraid of the crowd. He backed away across the stage.

"—should you make it through," a Lieutenant General in the front row said. A dozen adjutants flanked the seasoned UN commander. Enough brass stood up that a gold-and-green quilt rose to take the podium, rather than one man.

"You will be accorded as a hero, rotated back for recovery until the line needs you again. This soldier is trying to get the facts out, but hear me ladies and gentlemen: there is no quarter, there is no treaty. Kill or be killed."

That shut them up. Maybe I can eat now?

"Two weeks from now, we will begin our final offensive. Ground forces will push from now until then against the alien forces, pushing them to the easternmost tip of the Sahel zone. They will be supported by everything else we have in the remaining world's arsenal, short of vaporizing the planet.

"The survivors of this hard charge will be supplemented by my airborne troops here … and we will destroy every last vestige of their presence on our world. Ground Commanders, if you fail to secure these landing zones, all will be for naught. We do not have the resources for two of these operations. The battle will be designated 'Human Resolve.' It ends here, one way or another."

The Old Man went on for another hour. He talked about the strategic use of new incendiaries, tactics and big-picture stuff I didn't need to know. I was only fighting in one battle, on one front. I'm sure the guys in Nevada and Kashmir were facing the same tough calls, but I couldn't care about that. Our job was to secure the last pitched battle on the African continent. "Burn, shoot, chop, regroup." That was what I needed to know. The rest would come by osmosis and experience, provided I survived long enough. I left to get a sandwich and ended up with a hot redhead and a cold beer.

A crushing headache blurred my vision. I could not get enough breath into tightened lungs.

I came around under the shields. Becky and Grace were looking down at me. I heard Quinones' gears whirring close by.

"We thought we'd lost you, boss," Grace said.

"Took a nasty bit of debris to the head. You also had a talon stuck in your Kevlar. Would've been funny, a 'saur arm dangling from your head like a ponytail, if we didn't think he'd brained you first." Q towered over me.

Becky was the last of her replacement squad from the resupply in Congo. She was the best medic in the battalion, and she belonged to us. Becky's pre-war life was spent as a humanitarian in Doctors Without Borders, working as a nurse. Now, she was more of a mechanic than a philanthropist.

"Is he back?" Quinones asked. I heard him sucking down water.

It's got to be hot as hell in those things. I meant to say it, but my eyes just blinked instead.

"I'm alright. Give me a pill."

Becky looked to Grace for backup. "John. You sure? When was the last time you—"

"Pill," I said. I closed my eyes and sat up. When I opened them again, Grace stared at me. She gave me the pill, a mixture of stimulant, protein, and painkiller. She knew I lived on them now. I knew I would not live two more weeks on them. Like the General said, "Kill or be killed."

"We're not out of the woods yet, Boss," Grace said. "Your ticket is good for one more ride. Besides, we've got ourselves another new company commander to impress."

"We're here?" I tried to remember the last few hops. Memories of my family back in Virginia clawed at my consciousness, but the drugs shored up my psyche against those Elysian Fields.

"We are," Quinones said. His hands checked various munitions, while his eyes stood a vigilant watch. He scanned the terrain like a surveyor. Q would have made a good architect if his shot-put scholarship had been the only thing between him and college graduation.

Outside of the Shield-bearer's protective shields, AC-130H Spectre gunships unleashed fire like flying dragons. Thick swarms of prehistoric terror cleared away for the gliding clouds of the airborne division. Video feed from the coms gear showed a riling sea of 'saurs and islands of Jellies.

Each Spectre was stripped down to a fuselage bristling with firepower. Massive close air support systems designed specifically for fighting the 'saurs jutted out in all directions to lay waste to the enemy coming or going. In the massive depression the aliens now occupied, it was literally shooting in a barrel.

"That gear doesn't phase the Jellies much," I said. The drug's effect pulled me bodily into the moment.

"Are we going to make it?" Becky asked.

"We might evict 'em from Africa. I don't know about us."

"Is it actually hotter here?" Quinones said. Pebbles drifted down around his suit.

"Ever seen those monster movies, where they bring back dinosaurs? That's kind of what the Jellies are doing, but with the land," Becky said.

"Welcome to Jurassic—shit!" Quinones said. White phosphorous cordons burned out in front of the Shield-bearers' barrier.

"Let's go," I said. We ran out onto the flat-topped ledge and down into the fray.

The night was intermittently lit with explosions over the constant flames of pitched combat below. Paratroopers, vehicles, supply palates and flotsam crept downward like the Shadow Host. Soldiers were differentially drawn to the battle below—some out of fear, gravity and others bloodlust. No one could escape.

A flaming head, oddly akin to an Allosaur, careened by on the scorched earth behind me, digging a thin trench between me and the rest of the platoon.

"B-team, move up. A-team, hold."

"Boss—left flank," Private Quinones shouted, opening up with his arsenal.

Bless those 'Rat Traps,' I prayed to the heroes who had

manufactured the pneumatic rod exoskeleton. *Not much protection, but damn, what a load they can carry.* Five lizard torsos disintegrated before Quinones' withering fire.

"One-eighty!" I called out.

The two halves of my platoon regrouped, leaving an opening behind for the company commander and his men. The Shield-bearers surged. The partitions were up for us to shuttle through. We waited for the commander's order. A sinkhole in the ground behind us gave way as we turned in shock.

"Claymores. Now!" I cursed.

Those men—our entire command node and 73 more troops—were dead even if they did not know it yet. Close to home, the 'saurs used every trick their masters taught them. Soldiers from Becky's squad tossed belted explosives into the depths. Subterranean explosions covered us in dust and gore. The aliens tried to flank us from below and we buried them alive for their trouble.

Good boys.

"Surge!" I waived my arm overhead and ran full-tilt through the Shield-bearers' opening. I heard the earthmovers behind us fill the sinkhole with thermicrete.

"Boss, Major's dead. Everyone's dead," Becky said. She and Grace flanked me, picking off targets with M203 grenade launchers.

"It was going to happen. You know that. Keep on it," I yelled over our thundering guns. Switching barrels, I squeezed steel jacketed 10-guage slugs into a charging armored hulk.

"Je-sus. That looked like a triceratops," Grace yelled.

"Grace, take Becky. Check on ammo, get the wounded back under the shields. We can't afford to break now," I said, keeping my eyes on the horns as the 'saur thrashed, skidding headlong towards the shield-bearers.

"Roger. Becky. With me. Stay sharp," Grace said the last looking at me.

"Keep 'em away from ... the fires." I forgot myself as something like Ayer's rock hurtled toward us.

The ground rolled like an ocean. The grunts toughed it out, but the machinery took a hit. Evidently by the dissipating shells, so did the artillery. In prescient response, dozens of fighter-bombers dove like a cast of falcons.

"Sarge—Chinese?" Quinones took a knee behind me to watch, the pneumatics and gears hissed.

"Yeah, Panthers and Flankers I think. A couple of ours too ... maybe ... holy crap. Wild Weasels and frickin' Phantoms. Everybody down," I said.

The extreme low-altitude bombers tore a rift through the enemy ground force. As the shockwave of their wake hit, the shields lifted the entire battle engine off the ground like a sail. The aircrafts' guns blazed and rockeye bomblets bounced like Mardi Gras beads. A-10 Warthogs finished off the survivors as the animals turned to follow the first wave. The horizon erupted in flame behind the squadron.

Smells like a Texas barbeque. I took a deep breath in through my nose. We crouched on our haunches.

"Charge!" I said.

The platoon moved like a whip across the line as we shook off the bombing raid to take the smoldering ground. We crested the new, joined ellipses of impact craters in the glass-crusted sand.

I saw the titan Jelly formation. The air became hard to breathe, choked with smoke. 'Saurs gathered in huddles in the low ground ahead, dazed by the air attack. I took a knee to give the squads a chance to regroup.

"Check water, ammo, casualties," I said to my ... *company*.

I lifted infrared field glasses towards the towering amoebas in the distance.

Cold blooded or no, radiation does wonders for your body heat. I chuckled.

"They may be retreating. Hold your ground. No one passes us," I commanded. "Get ready."

As if on cue, all manner of carnivorous murderer turned their necks our direction. The hellish denizens waved back and forth, surveyed the immense line of Human Resolve. My team leaders shouted as the wave began.

We fanned out down to our last drum of shells.

Becky rushed over. "Boss, the chutes. In the dark, just past the WP. The troopers!"

They fired over our heads. We dropped prone, my soldiers kept up the perimeter until the airborne touched down. Their fire came in staccato waves as boots hit the ground. The reinforcements stepped in and knelt between us.

"Howdy pardner," an enormous Scot dropped a duffle bag of ammo cans next to me. "Thought you Yanks could use a break."

His grin shone in the darkness around us, flickering by the white phorphorous blaze and gunfire. The array of humanity strung around the perimeter of the aliens' glut turned into a Maginot Line ten guns deep. Division after division filled in between our advanced ground units and Engineers.

I heard the B1s pulling through before the blast hit us.

Our Last Stand

Well-rehearsed drills quieted our guns, folding us as we took refuge behind whatever was close by. Cries and shouts erupted as distracted soldiers' vision was obliterated by nuclear fire.

"Low-yield bombs. I'd probably look like my own grandma if they were regular ones, eh Grace?" Becky said from a gaggle of troops a few yards over.

"After all this desert, what makes you think you don't already, chicka?" Q shouted back.

"First wave didn't get very close. Those guys need a distraction to get the job done," I said. I thought about my family. My kids back in Virginia, growing their own vegetables to survive. About my wife and how lonely things might get for her.

"What are you thinking boss?" Grace asked.

I couldn't look her in the face.

"This is it, isn't it? Time to put it to bed." Quinones stood watch over us, scanning the battle through his monitors to protect his eyes from the radiation.

"Your family's still waiting for you. I'll do it, just tell me what to do." Gracie said.

"No gas," I said. "You know that I'm not going to tell you to do something and not do it myself."

I could tell she was pissed. It was the look you reserved for a brother or sister when they give you a slap in the face only siblings could muster, throwing your secrets at you like knives.

"Get off it. Guys, we're going to hijack that artillery truck. The one with the fat microwave array. Then we're going to drive it straight into the Jellies," I said.

"They'll smash us before we get close enough to hit 'em," Q said.

"Only if we come in guns-a-blazin'," I said. "We're going to drive up to their knees and give 'em a big kick."

"They don't have knees, or skeletons for that matter." Becky said, coming late to the huddle.

"Don't worry about that, Sergeant." Faster than she could react, I pinned my stripes to her Kevlar and armor. "Now. Go carry on. You've got to report a theft. We've got 20 minutes till the next run."

"What?"

"Just go." Grace wrapped her arms around Becky, said something I couldn't catch and hurled her from us towards the command post at the rear. Becky stumbled, but unsure of what else to do, walked on as ordered, like a shamed golden retriever.

"What about the gas?" Quinones asked.

"We use our rebreather masks, like the Navy guys showed us," I said.

"What about after the 20 minutes they're good for? Or the seals on the truck? Those alien farts eat right through them when it's thick."

I just looked him in the eye.

"Right," he said. I'll go get us the truck."

"I heard that Puerto Ricans have a knack for that sort of thing."

Q just smiled, flashed some teeth and stepped away.

"The last hurrah," Grace said. She oozed contempt and resignation.

"Let's make up for Frisco, eh? I asked. A little smile barely creased the edges of her lips.

We stepped into the self propelled artillery cab as two drivers shook their heads and walked away. Who'd want to steal a microwave cannon that would protect you from the boulders sure to arrive after that wave? It made as much sense as stealing a fire truck in the middle of a wildfire. Once the drivers were absorbed by the crowd, Quinones shrugged off his suit using the emergency releases, then manned the weapons station. Grace and I climbed up into the cabin, crawling up the nine-foot-tall off-road tires.

"Get your masks ready," I said, releasing the parking brake. The lumbering truck broke formation. The cab's communications erupted in orders to return. "Uh, everything's under control. Situation normal. Uh, we had a slight weapons malfunction …"

The fire control officers continued to yell back on the radio. Grace cut the radio's microphone wire with her knife. "Boring conversation."

"I always wanted to say that. Thanks," I said. In the short span, the truck broke past the last of the human line. We were close enough to the aliens that they were all we could see. We were giggling like high school pranksters.

"Hey guys, if you're done monkeying around up there, I can barely get a breath in."

Grace checked the environmental gauges. "Q, I'm pumping all the air reserves to you. Hopefully that pushes out the seals. The alien farts are eating through the gaskets and we're about compromised. I'm locking you down in the turret. It'll protect you longer having a hard seal after ours."

"Grace. Get your mask on."

"Ain't gonna happen, Sarge. You need to stay conscious long enough to get us into the thick of them. You're going to use my mask, once yours is out. The radiation's already killed us all. Can't be for nothin'."

She leaned against the doorframe and looked out at something I could not see. Grace pulled her hair out of its bun. Clumps came with it, falling like wheat chaff on her beaten uniform. She sighed, reliving a happier memory.

We finally approached one of the Jellies' pseudopods. Grace reached for my hand, not turning her head.

"Now?" Q asked. He coughed so hard I heard it through the cabin rather than just the intercom.

"Not yet. If we get bogged down then do it. I'm going to try to pass through." The engines' pitch rose and the nose of the truck dove as we hit the outer membrane. Then it gave and we slid through.

"Like butter," he said.

"Like a beach assault." We popped out the other side and into another, and another. Grace's face was hidden in the crook of her arm, held up by the seat harness. She looked like she fell asleep on a long road trip. I knew better. I was wearing he mask and it was almost depleted. The seal was giving way to the corrosives that already ate through my exposed skin and past the nerve endings.

"Q ... all directions, full power ... after next ... pocket. Burn ... burn it all."

"Sir, pri—Sergeant Hanni reporting from the front line."

"What is it, Sergeant?" The Major who vetted the incoming reports never looked away from his screen, his hands were a blur with activity, organizing and forwarding data.

"Sir, a SPARTY microwave cannon has been hijacked. It's heading straight into the Jellies."

"Doesn't matter now. They're cooked. More incoming missiles on their way. These from silos in Kansas. Even if those bastards can pop 'em back like fly balls, they can't hit all of them. We'll just have to push through. Ready your men for the ground assault, Sergeant."

"Yes sir." Becky left the command post in a daze. People scrambled machinery around her, shouting obscentities. Her eyes were transfixed above the horizon. The Jellies loomed in the distance. Towering masses of wavering amoebic flesh quivered and exploded from the inside out, without the air strike's help.

Thin trails of tears traced through the dust on her face. The Jellies flattened like wrestlers pinning an opponent. Wave after wave rose and fell on the same stretch of earth. The shockwaves unsettled the dunes between her and the front, almost like the Earth gave her a direct view to the battle. She heard the odd, screeching roar of the missiles overhead. Their jets were pushing the air from her lungs, even at this distance. None of the nukes were tossed back this time. No need to hurry.

12

Everything Old is New Again

"SO, NOT only did Slim not bring extra sun screen, he didn't even bother to ask for some when we finally hit the pool," Hero said. The group of soldiers gathered around the campfire winced.

"No wonder he's in the infirmary," a voice in the crowd said.

"Yeah, the blisters just keep showing up, no matter how many get lanced. It's medieval just to watch him put on a t-shirt," Carter said.

"Did Ish give him an article?" a female soldier from another section asked.

"Yeah, but I don't think it'll go all the way through. Sergeant Major will probably see it as punishment enough. Besides, there isn't any work to do other than daily. We ain't even doing official roll calls," Hero said.

"Damn. So who won the contest?" the same woman asked.

"Doesn't really matter," Tom said.

"Another song?" Hero asked.

"All Along the Watchtower," Chance shouted.

"You shold've been here an hour ago, friend. Already played that one. Sorry," Hero said.

"And, I do believe it's time to light these up," Carter said. "Last song."

Hero flicked her 1940's era Zippo and held it for Carter after lighting her own Monte Cristo *No. 1* cigar.

"Can we say *mission accomplished?*" Hero said. She blew a series of smoke rings in the firelight.

Everyone laughed, knowing they would be here again.

"What's that guy's name, you know, Jacob? Don Marley? Bob McClean?" Carter asked.

"Dude, I think you've got Bob Marley confused with 'A Christmas Carol.' Like some Rastafarian ghost dragging his chains intead of dreadlocks." Hero shook her head side to side, "Ching-ching-clang, *Hey mon …*"

Carter laughed so hard tears started to run down his cheek. "Don McClean. That's it. Everyone got some room for 'Pie?'"

The crowd joined in, smoking like an Iraqi oil field. Some of them had followed their fathers' footprints past the rusted hulks of the Republican Guard's tank lines just days before. Emotions ran the gamut of the song's lyrics.

"…Do you recall what was revealed, the day, the music died—" sang the crowd to Hero and Carter's straining guitars.

"HEY!" shouted Sergeant Tweed. The self-proclaimed only "real" soldier in their ranks, he'd come from the 101st Airborne Infantry for this deployment. He was also coincidentally the most high-strung guy in the unit. "Go to bed. Kill the music. If you haven't dispersed before I get out of the tent, you'll get written up!"

Tweed was caught between a universal joke and being the

management's whipping boy. The group dispersed, ridiculous cockcrows erupted from the shadows. Safely watching from the USO tent, Carter and Hero slaked their raspy voices and watched Tweed poke about in the darkness.

"Well, we had a Five o'clock Charlie, might as well have a Burns, yeah?" Hero said.

"Does that make me Hawkeye or BJ? Funny how he made us quit on that line," Carter said.

Sergeant Tweed tripped on a guy wire, shaking an officers' tent. Soon he was face down in the dirt doing push-ups.

"Don't think he'd see the irony." Hero put out her butt in the dust and recycled her can.

We do not know today whether we are busy or idle. In times when we thought ourselves indolent we had discovered afterward that much was accomplished and much was begun in us.
Ralph Waldo Emerson

As a special bonus for the collected edition of "Adventures in the Fantastic," here is a story that has never before been in print.

13

Bits and Pieces

GEORGE sat in a very worn leather armchair under the critical gaze of his ancestors' portraits around the room. Unopened bills and creditor solicitations littered the reading room's floor. He could hear the old house creak, as the mortuary and living quarters were still one structure.

One of George's hands held two fingers of Glenmorangie. The other cradled a video connection to his longtime girlfriend, Liz. A first edition "The House of Usher" sat open on his lap, a derelict of time spent before she joined him. The Tiffany lamp on the telephone table next to the chair gave just enough light she could see his hangdog expression. It laid almost comical, drawn on his thin, cartoonish face and silver close-cropped Caesar haircut.

"Don't you think that's a little dramatic?" Liz asked.

George sighed. "Okay, so the plaster on the walls isn't falling down."

"...and you don't have a sister or lover in the basement, and the whole place isn't sinking into some swampy moat."

"I get it. Geez." George said.

"Just get off your butt and do some repairs. There's plenty of video ref's on the net. It'll do the place some good and get you out of this funk. You don't want to be the cliché mortician, all walking cadaver."

George drained his glass. He wiped his lips with his finger and thumb. He paused long enough to soak up the little bit of liquor that clung to them.

"You're right. They just got under my skin," George said.

"So you don't think there's a conspiracy?" Liz said.

George sighed. "Not really. Sherman and Sons is just a money grubbing corporation. Just the mechanics of business. Shoulda' stayed in school."

"Have another drink, love. Call me in the morning."

"Can do, Ms. Lancaster. G'night."

Liz's final image was a perfect Varga girl kiss. Some animal stirred in George, then went back to sleep. He poured another drink and turned up Beethoven's Moonlight Sonata.

"How's this for cliché, doll?" George fidgeted uncontrollably, trying to shake the arrhythmia and shortness of breath intrusive thoughts of Sherman & Sons brought him.

George woke with a snort as the doorbell's video link rang under his thigh. Sunshine streamed through the odd, canted triangular windows in the eaves of the sitting room. It flashed him in the eyes. Startled, George almost fell out of the leather armchair as he knocked his half full whisky glass to the floor.

"Damn." He blotted the booze from the hand knotted rug with yesterday's undershirt.

"Hello?" George stammered to gain composure and angle the camera away from his bare chest.

"Mr. Barstow? Sorry to disturb you so early in the morning. May we come in?" A woman in a severe suit asked. Two men with briefcases accompanied her. George cleared his throat.

"Just give me a second, please." George said.

He left the shirt to soak up the spill, nicked a clean gray t-shirt from a nearby linen drawer on his way through the mahogany paneled automatic door. George hurried down the hallway to the front door of the living side of the house.

"These corporate robber barons presume to use *my* door? It *is* personal." George stopped a moment to straighten his hair and smoothe his chinos before he answered the door.

"Hello?" George said again.

"Mr. Barstow. Kitty Kelly of Sheman and Sons Services. These are my associates Mr. Gladys and Mr. Helen."

Kitty's grip was as final as Death itself. George was happy when she relented.

"Mr. Barstow. May we come in?" she said.

There was no pause, and the question came out like a statement. The other men were silent hulks in charcoal gray suits. The muscle followed like bookends in a corporate buyout sandwich.

"She really said that?" Liz asked.

"Honest to Anubis. 'We were sorry to hear about the loss of accounts here at Barstow.' That cow knows I know she went hunting for my clients and undersold me. Doesn't matter that their funerals won't cover their expenses, they have shops around the country to pick up the slack," George said.

"Maybe there's some side work you could expand into to make ends meet? I mean, what about a deal with the coroner?

Or a medical college? Hell, even redecorating the reception room for parties …"

George took a breath before answering. They had this conversation every other day it seemed. "You're right hon. As always. I'll start looking around. Want to come with me?" George said. He stood up and walked to the door.

"Right now? I've got clients of my own to get to sweetie. I wouldn't be ready before you got here. Let me know how it turns out? Happy hunting."

George put on a thin windbreaker and a pair of penny loafers. He stopped in the kitchen on his way out to fill up a travel coffee mug. The phone rang.

"Is this Barstow Funerary?" an old man asked.

"Yes. This is George Barstow. How may we help you?" George said.

"I am afraid my daughter is dead."

"Our condolences in your time of loss, sir. Would you like to come in or have us visit you?" George asked.

"You took care of my late father and wife in their time. Will you meet me at the coroner's office? I could use some support."

"Absolutely. Can I have your last name?" George adapted into his professional mask. A smile covered the frustration and turmoil from his talk with Liz.

"Kortsen. Carl Kortsen."

"Mr. Kortsen, again may I offer you our condolences on your loss. We are happy to serve your family again, sir. What time may we join you?"

"I am being driven there now. I hope that's not too much trouble?"

"Not at all, not for an old friend of the family. I will meet you shortly."

Carl Kortsen's daughter Molly was forty-two. She had work done to the point George half expected zippers under her chin and arms. The work was excellent, no visible scars except to the trained eye and the fact that there was no blood flush to mask them.

"Sherman and Sons didn't get you, eh Pretty?" George said. He worked hard to keep up his professional face, lest he was caught with his proverbial pants down over this win.

The mortuary's workroom was otherwise empty as George clipped the sutures open along her Y-incision. The coroner had neatly replaced the internal organs so that they made a sort of composite smiley face in the cavity. George chuckled.

"That's what you do in this business. A personal touch. Leave the corporate coldness to the grave."

The doorbell rang. George took off his gloves and checked his display. A short, squat man in a shiny suit tried to peer through the peephole from the outside in.

"Why do I even think people will use the business door anymore?" George said. He huffed and in a puerile fit knocked over a tray of tools for spite.

He answered the video link.

The short, pudgy man made himself at home at George's kitchen table. His name was Joe Sonoita, a sawbones on retainer with the local Russian mob and half of the city's street gangs. Joe was unassuming, like a fat kid who was picked on at school. If you watched his eyes though, they belied a fox rather than a beaten puppy. Joe constantly watched for an advantage or a new angle. Everyone knew he was for sale. No one trusted him with more than the task at hand. Once upon a time, he played fast and loose with his medical license. Joe lost it after several scandals broke at once involving misconduct and unprofessional behavior. George often wondered what he did that made those charges stick in this day and age. Still, Joe was a known person in town. He offered fringe medical services on-site and rumors abounded of his non-listed services.

George still wore his work clothes and there were embalming fluid stains on his apron. He tried not to be huffy. The disgraced doctor across from him said he had some side work available at the door. George was aware of the tax due on the family business and the lack of funds in the bank. The stiff chick meant cool cash, enough to keep the lights on and the fridge full, but not much else. Sherman & Sons' embargo was taking a serious toll. Every other private mortuary now owed its name to a corporate parent, Sherman & Sons Services. They offered their clients cut rate deals until the competition was gone and then charged whatever they wanted. Families suffered. The mortician's first, as their businesses failed. Then the survivors, as they were charged exorbitant fees for cut-rate services to offset Sherman and Sons' bidding war with local mortuaries elsewhere. The Barstow family had always been keen investors, and they had a long history in Portland before it was even incorporated. George was a good custodian, but there were more bills to pay than the annuities could afford on their own. Sherman and Sons was draining him like a fresh corpse—slowly.

"There. Now, Joe, was it? What is the offer? I'm a little busy," George said.

"I heard about Kitty Kelly and the late Ms. Kortsen. Thought I might be able to help you out." Joe said.

"Joe Sonoita. Last I heard you were operating out of an SUV."

"It has a trailer, and it's a big SUV. My clients prefer discretion and house calls."

"Or lack of a house calls." George said.

"If you don't want to get back on your feet, I'll leave you to your guest," Joe said. He raided the fridge for a jar of olives.

George relented. "So, what is it?"

"Things must really be that bad then. Okay. I need a bunch of breasts."

"Excuse me?" George said. At six-foot-two, he towered over the impish man.

"Implants. All types actually, not just breasts. You get some in here, I'll pay nicely. Fill the cadavers with old socks or something."

"No wonder you lost your license," George said.

"Fine, see you on the streets then pal," Joe said.

Joe walked to the front door. George reached over him and stopped the door with his hand.

"How much?" George said.

"Kortsen has some. Make me a cuppa, go down and get 'em. I'll give you two G's right here."

George closed his eyes and took a few breaths. The hairs on the back of his neck and arms stood up. He looked like he was choking back on the urge to vomit. George opened his eyes, was about to say something, then his glance fell to a fresh stack of collection notices. Defeated before he began, George's composure collapsed.

"Fine," he said.

George put a kettle on and threw a packet of Earl Grey into a chipped saucer. He took the long way down to the workroom. The portraits of the last four owners of the mortuary stared at him in shame. He stopped along the narrow passage, almost in synch with the tintypes and photos. Twice he turned a little to double back. Lights were on in the last three workrooms. George did not remember using them, with business as slow as it was. Something distracted him. George shuffled on, closed the door to the worktable area behind him as if to escape their notice. The gloves slapped against his wrists, then made wet, squelchy noises as he felt up Molly Kortsen in a way only the coroner had before.

"I'm sorry," he said. George could not tear his eyes from her deflated flesh while the rinse station warmed up. George turned his back to her body, he felt her icy stare pierce his brain across the small room. He tried to avoid Molly's misty gaze as he walked out of the room and upstairs with the silicone gel impants, but her disdain was inescapable even up to the kitchen.

Joe sipped his tea. George plopped down the two plastic bags in front of him. He fell into a chair opposite, obviously haggard.

"What? No bag?" Joe said. "Never mind. Next time."

Joe threw three piles of wrinkled bills onto the table. He slipped the breast implants into his jacket pockets.

"*Call me when you get more. Or anything else I can reuse. Guess we're both going green, eh?*" Joe said.

As the door closed behind Joe, George dropped face first into the ancient Formica of his kitchen table.

Joe walked up to the the delivery entrance pulling a flatbed cart covered with a lumpy tarp. The rain washed away ichor into the gutter before it became a pool of bodily fluids at George's doorstep. He rang the bell. George answered the door in person, sliding the screeching metal double doors aside.

"These guys didn't make it," Joe said. "You know, a little maintenance would get rid of that noise …"

"Did they die before or after you got a hold of them?" George said.

"Funny. I thought I was doin' you a favor."

"So did they, I bet." He wheeled the gurney stacked with bodies down the basement's ramp.

"Things are looking better in here, George. Glad to see you're not spending the money on hookers and blow."

"Bills are paid up. Building back the hard times bulwarks," George said.

"And I want to make sure you get ahead. Say, you been stockpiling again?"

The secured shelf of embalming fluid and hazardous chemicals looked crowded.

"Before I knew you, I had no idea that this stuff was popular. Dangerous. I guess no more dangerous than the other stuff kids shove up their noses, smoke, and what."

"Yeah, and as long as you keep logging the bodies no one's the wise without exhuming them. Fat chance any jury's gonna be so interested in the whereabouts of folks like these." Joe kicked the body-laden gurney. "Anything you salvage let me know. In the meantime, I'll take six pints of juice."

George put on his gloves and took out six pints of embalming fluid. He knew without fingerprints it was circumstantial if the jars were traced back to him. For good measure, he gave them a wipe down with a chlorhexadine towel.

"Here's your cut. Might suggest getting a designer to redecorate the upstairs. It's like a mausoleum," Joe said. "You interested in some more side work?"

George fell into a waste bucket and vomited. He stood up again in a moment, wiping his face with another towel. He looked as drained as Molly had two days earlier.

"In for a penny …" George said. He stooped over the waste bucket again.

Joe sat in a high stool with the operating room light shone behind him like a halo.

"I hate it when you do that," George said.

"Fine," Joe said. He stayed put. "You know that crack I made about people not snooping around for these guys?"

"Yeah …"

"There's a lot of folks that no one would mind missing. Everybody's got a worth of some kind. Maybe some's just breathing." Joe said.

George's blank face was a mask.

"Did you ever hear what my specialty was back in the day?" Joe said.

"Colon & Rectal surgery?"

"Close. I was a dual specialist, plastic and transplants."

"Dead tissue is dead-dead by the time it gets to me, Dr. West," George said.

"What about slightly fresher? Skin can be grafted from either alive or cadaver donors. People literally have extra veins and arteries in their legs," Joe said.

A long pregnant pause hung in the musty basement air between them. George crumbled a little more.

"Call me Roderick … You'd have to show me," George said.

"No problem. How about this fella here?"

"What? Now?" George asked.

"Got plans, have you? I can make it worth your while," Joe said.

George pushed off from the cabinet he leaned against. He donned his work clothes and apron. From a drawer in the cabinet he withdrew a tray of sterilized mortuary tools under a hermetic plastic cover.

"Let's get to work. We're going to need your usual I.V. solution, or saline. Distilled water will work in a pinch. Oh, and lots of ice."

"No problem in a morgue," George said.

He prepared buckets of solution and an ice bath for them in the oversized sink. In an hour, he was twenty thousand dollars richer and vomiting into the now empty sink. Joe demonstrated how to extract veins, arteries and how to remove useable skin for transplant.

"There's a lot of burn victims who would be happier with this than pig skin," Joe said.

"The money is insane—who pays this much for used implants when new ones are the same or less? Or cadaver grafts?"

Joe was silent.

George was too deep in self-loathing depression to ask what the veins and arteries were for. The obscenity of the over-large bankroll kicked him in the crotch every time he saw it.

George stopped at a vacant lot next to the restaurant. "I'm going to tell her. She should know," he said. "We're a team."

He took a piece of string from his worn scarf and set about the weeds and rushes. A few quick cuts with his pocketknife and a boquet of wild flowers appeared in his hand. George kicked the mud and dew from his oxfords on the sidewalk and strode into the Vietnamese bistro.

Adventures in the Fantastic

It was Wednesday. He and Liz took a break from their work to catch up face to face. After so many months, George still looked forward to these routine dates. A little brass bell chimed above the door when George entered. His heart beat a little faster. The heat assailed him in a wave. Dressed in his long coat, George felt his body try to adjust by pumping all the excess through his face.

"I … I can't do it," he said to himself.

He began to sweat. Liz waived to him from a booth at the back of the dining room. George hung his coat and scarf on the communal coat rack. He passed the flowers from hand to hand with care and tried to catch his sudden loss of breath.

"Hi sweetie," Liz said.

George kissed her and handed over the bunch of purple, blue, yellow and brown flowers accented with thistle and blackberry buds.

"Ready to order?" George said.

"Absolutely."

When the food arrived, they were deep into the events of Liz's day. George held both of Liz's hands across the table. As the waitress set the platters down, George moved the two dinner plates to his side of the U-shaped booth. She gave him a bat of her eyelashes and scooted in close.

George arrived home to his front door ajar. His heart pounded as he snuck up to the stoop. He listened. Joe's laughter assaulted his ears, and he could smell an off-brand of humanity drift from inside. A mad man's cackle joined Joe's as George kicked the door the rest of the way open.

"What the hell are you at in my kitchen!" he said.

"Just a spot of tea, a double deal," Joe said.

A homeless man in a wheel chair ate a loaf of George's white bread. He cradled the plastic sleeve between his knees.

"Name's Jack. I hear you've got a bit of an operation here?" he said.

"Jack here has offered us some living tissue, special order veins and arteries for a client who wants to ... boost his standing with the ladies," Joe said.

"As you can see, I ain't exactly usin' mine. Either way," Jack said.

"Okay ... Joe, wanna help me prep downstairs?" George asked. Jack laughed.

"Be right back," Joe said to Jack as he and George walked through the vestibule towards the staircase.

"What the hell! This is not a spare parts lab for you, pal," George said. He held Joe by his shirt stays against the wall. George's ancestors' portraits glared in the short hallway.

"Easy, Roderick. I'm just helping you out. This will pay more, open more opportunities for you and get you in good with clients who come back. Something I know you're not exactly familiar with. It's as easy as a cadaver, we can use insulin and ether to make it just so. I'll take the bits with me and Jack, give him a lift back home, and we all come out better for it. Just take it easy."

George sighed and shambled down into the basement workroom. Just as before, Joe instructed while George performed the operation. It was surprisingly easy work. George worked up the courage by the end of the procedure to corner Joe again.

"Tell me straight now. What are you doing with his ... pieces?" George asked.

"Nothing sinister. I wasn't kidding about the burns. A lot of guys find themselves on fire in my clients list. I don't ask how."

"And the blood vessels? There's way more here than you'd

need for that, plus skin is fed by capillaries, not these giants," George said.

"You know, legs have a lot of interesting differences compared to other parts of the body. The blood vessels here have little semi-valve like structures, keeps the blood flowing evenly up and down. Of course, that's not terribly unusual, another limb does that too—" Joe said.

"—You're using his leg's blood vessels for penile enlargement?" George said.

Joe chaffed. "Those pills are just flim-flam by comparison."

"There'd be all kinds of tissue rejection—"

"—These are the guys who are injecting silicone to give them a leg up," Joe said.

"Only to have it fall off from complications? Or because the tissue's not designed to do what you're doing?"

"They don't care. Actually, they care, they care about the need and not the long term. Hell, most of these guys are toast soon after seeing me anyhow."

"Coincidence?" George asked.

"Besides, everyone is making out fine and happy but you sour pus," Joe said. "You want to do some actual good? Then let's talk organs. I've got anti-rejection meds that'll—"

"No," George said. "No, no, no. Absolutely not. Take your donor home, get out of my house."

Two weeks passed in a haze. Joe's money made a real difference. It still gnawed at him like an ulcer through his entire body. Tuesday, the business doorbell rang. George almost fell over. He checked the monitor on his mobile. *Kitty Kelly. Sherman and Sons.*

"Can I come in? It's just me," she said.

George selected the option to record her visit from his device. He opened the double doors wide.

"What do you want?" George said.

"Sorry, I heard you were having a hard time, but I see that I'm mistaken." She inventoried the newly refurnished entry. "Love the new wallpaper. Did you change florists?" Ms. Kelly said.

"Let me say it again. What do you want?"

Kitty looked around the room's portraits of the previous mortician-operators. They all seemed to scowl, judging their meeting with disgust.

"To make you another offer. We can end these stresses now. You can keep your family home. You don't have to join us or sell out. Just stop doing the business. We can give you a good nest egg to find something else. Surely you were pressured into this life. I am offering a way of doing what you want to do, George."

"That easy, huh?" George said.

"I have the papers and a check with lots of zeroes right here."

"And that's it? I stay independent, you go away, just give up?"

"Not give up, George. Prove you're as smart as I know you are," Kitty said.

"How many zeroes?"

"Six. Not including the pennies."

George moved to take a pen from his pocket. He hesitated and dropped his hands back to his waist. Kitty did not bother to hide her disappointment.

"Are all people commodities nowadays?"

"Everyone is, sooner or later, George."

"Please, Kitty. It's infuriating when you pretend to be a friend. We have helped our actual friends here for over a century. By comparison, Sherman and Sons is a fad."

"Most people just want a good deal," Kitty said.

"I for one am not a whore. Now, please, leave me alone." George said.

Kitty clasped her valise with a crash of metal on metal. She stood, smoothed her Chanel skirt and walked to the door. Kitty turned slightly, held a calla lily to her nose. While it framed her lips towards George she mouthed, "You're finished," and smiled.

George ran after her. He slammed the doors shut instead of flying out into the street. The automatic hinges slowed them just enough to keep them from banging together. He held his hands up in front of him along the shared doorjamb and rested his face against his forearms.

Kitty's sedan drove away at a creep. The beat up van across the street rocked a little.

George wandered downtown, mixing with the homeless men in military surplus clothing. His own suit and overcoat looked dingy and worn. He blended right in. The hours passed. George lost track of time and the reason he avoided home. The day turned to evening, and George meandered the way the Portland neighborhoods did, sometimes walking a fringe of businesses and houses shuffled together. Everything and nothing made sense as he watched minutes stretch then snap forward like a rubber band. He looked as bedraggled as a Great Dane's favorite toy.

"Wednesday again?" Roderick said. They walked in the street. Cars honked and swerved around. No one got out to scold George though.

"Skipped the last two dates," George said.

"We're late." Roderick said.

The weather was colder than normal. The rain would make it worse. It might freeze.

"Might make it better for business," Roderick said.

"Like we do that sort of trade anymore."

The restaurant door opened. Garlic and wine smells drifted out and George forced himself in.

"We're about to close, sir," the hostess said.

"I see my girlfriend over there. Can I at least join her?" George said. He did not wait for a reply.

Liz sat alone, a busboy cleaned the tables nearby.

"Where have you been?" Liz said. "Did you forget it was …"

"Just got derailed. Sorry," George said.

"Three weeks in a row. That's a bit much, George," she said.

"Sorry."

"Are you getting bored? I know work's hard … Sherman and Sons …"

"No! I … just—"

Liz wiped her lipstick off on a napkin. "Tell you what. Next week you make me dinner at the house. I'll see if I can keep you from getting bored or derailed?"

Liz had already paid her bill. She gathered her purse, coat and hat. Liz brushed past a hunched George. She headed for the door.

"A bottle of Lambrusco, please?" Roderick said to the busboy.

A minute later, only the barest of lights were on. The busboy almost dropped the wine bottle and glass into George's lap. The hostess flirted with the busboy. He laughed as the dressed up girl hit on the work stained kid. The TV was on in the kitchen. The boy retreated, without a glance at George. He started to pour.

"Flirt," Roderick said.

George wandered aimlessly through the streets. Local kids played. People got on and off busses and trams. Amid the hustle and bustle, George's focus was blurred. He could not bring a single face into detail. Their movements were clipped. George stared into an offbeat zoetrope through cataracts. The effect made him nauseous. He puked on the sidewalk. It dribbled down his coat. People averted their eyes and stayed out of reach. He argued with himself.

"You're not that smart," George said.

"They'll find out. They'll find you. Then what?" Roderick said.

"He's trying to expose you. He's going to get you caught."

"That woman. Naw, not her, the other one," Roderick said. "She's not going to stop. She'll ruin you."

"Us."

"Something has to be done."

"Who are we to decide the value of a life? They might be saved. We're murdering them if we don't try," George said.

"They're dead already. *He* wouldn't be involved if they weren't. Decent people don't use back alley physicians," Roderick said.

"A life is a life. We deal with the dead," George said.

"Exactly."

Dawn broke to find George huddled behind trashcans in an alley next to a used bookstore and second-hand clothier. The rains came again in the night, further stained his abused garments. He sniffed the air with its fecund earth undertone and piney top-not so abundant through the width and breadth of the Willamette valley. The ground squelched beneath his feet. George drew his mobile and called for a cab home.

The stoop creaked under his weight. The lit entryway belied

a darkened house. George put a kettle on the gas stove, stripped and washed in the kitchen sink. The kettle whistled, then piped down as George poured the water into a cup, followed by a sachet filled with black tea and aromatics. Tea this way was a holdover from his days away from home, when he traveled around the world at his parents' behest. They wanted him to feel like he experienced all that the world could offer a young man of his status. They knew full well he would return to the family business once away from its succor. Tears came without notice. George stood naked at the sink, drank his tea. He made a sandwich to soothe his conscience. George's grandmother, Wanda, had been a southern belle. Death and dying were important facets of their culture too. She was always a comfort. Wanda said that the funerals were for the living, and that it was important to remember the dead while we lived on. George put the dishes in the sink and took a proper shower to draw the chill from his bones if not his soul. The phone rang as George pulled his trousers from the hanger.

"Hi Joe. What do you need for the process?" George asked. "Yeah, well it makes sense. I'll have it ready after today."

George lounged in the sitting room. He admired the molded tin ceiling over a rocks glass of whisky. The over-filled glass sloshed as he sat up. Someone banged on the cargo entrance doors to the basement. He heard the back-up warning of a delivery truck. George splashed single-malt as he held on to the drink and ran downstairs.

"Dear god …" George said. His drink was gone in a gulp.

"*Morning, sunshine.*" Joe picked up a clipboard.

A thick Russian voice called out over the engine noise. Joe

scribbled on the pad and handed it up to the driver. A pair of men in designer suits opened the container from the inside. Their tattoos peeked out from the cuffs and collars of their jackets. George froze. Joe took a hand and climbed up to meet them. George could hear them just audible over the exhaust.

"*She's still breathing ...*" Joe said.

A flash and three pops slapped Joe's eyes and ears inside the truck's cargo hold.

"*Okay. Never mind,*" Joe said as he hopped down. The men in the truck unloaded three cardboard boxes.

"*Where do you want them, all in the workroom?*"

"Sure," George said.

The three men in the cab closed the doors and the panel truck roared away. There was a light mist that made George shiver. Roderick followed Joe inside.

"*Scrub up, make sure to get under your nails,*" Joe said.

The hot water foamed against the soap on George's forearms.

"It's a good decision, George," Roderick muttered to himself.

"Don't you start," George whispered back.

"*Did you say somethin'? Hey, remember when you used to be a mortician?*" Joe said.

Roderick and Joe laughed. George gripped the sink in rage.

"This is really good, sweetie," Liz said. "The noodles, you said you made them? Amazing!"

"Thanks," George said.

Roderick scrubbed dishes in the kitchen's sink.

"I'm glad we stayed in tonight," Liz said.

George stuck to the dishes.

"Wanna go do something crazy?" Liz said.

"Sure," Roderick said.

"I've got something in my pocket."

"Me too," Roderick said with a grin.

"I'll be right back. Meet me in the display room and you can show me yours."

"Deal," Roderick said. George dried the dishes and put them in the cupboard. He produced an insulin pen and removed the safety cap. Liz was not quiet about her arrival in the casket showroom. Roderick walked in.

"How about some role playing, something naughty?" Liz said. She knelt inside a gothic coffin. It was black lacquer, a quileted red velvet liner. She wore a black veil that reached her black-and-red lace demi-cups. A matched thong pulled into a "Y" hid behind the bent line of the casket.

"How about a step closer to the edge?" Roderick held up the syringe.

Liz shook out her hair beneath the veil. She stretched out sideways and offered her arm. Roderick took her by the bicep, traced the pen tip down her skin to her belly, and with a click he was done. Liz's head soon lolled against the plush coffin interior.

"Shhh ..." Roderick said.

He felt her pulse become thready. Roderick watched her lungs struggle. Her eyes dilated. He tilted her head to the side when she vomited. She lost control of her body and began to seize.

George ran to the kitchen, grabbed a plastic funnel and poured corn syrup into her mouth.

"Fine!" Roderick screamed. George forced her to swallow.

George waited until her body recovered and ran into the

sitting room. Roderick beat George unconscious and dragged him back into the coffin with Liz. She woke with the sunrise.

Liz screamed. George could not open his eyes or breathe through his nose. The casket fell off the stand and the lid pinned him to the ground. Liz scrambled out the wedged opening and ran into the street.

George overcame the pain of the crushed and pinned arm. The coffin door slapped him bodily as he pushed against the bed. After a struggle, he toppled it over and away. Roderick found his phone and dialed emergency services.

"—ockingbird lane," George said.

"Help is on the way," the operator said.

As he lost consciousness, George saw Liz helped into a cab by men in coveralls. They got back into the van that was always parked down the street now. The men did not drive away. They continued to watch.

"Sherman and Sons have been watching this whole time. That bi—" Roderick growled.

Joe appeared in the front door, silhouetted by the daylight.

"Jesus!" Joe said.

"I hate it when you do tha …" George said. He passed out.

George woke in a hospital bed. He was tied down with heavy leather restraints. He felt a significant beard on his face. A policeman stood outside the door. The cop, alerted by the feedback tones from the diagnostic machines in George's room, picked up the radio mic from his shoulder. He did not come in. The nurse left him alone. Eventually the beeps silenced themselves. George was left to flashbacks of what brought him in. He could not see for the tears that streamed down his temples. He choked on his own vomit.

Time passed. It seemed like an eternity. George was poked and prodded. No one spoke to him. A psychiatrist sat him upright and administered visual tests through a headset. He stayed silent as he fiddled with his machine and the display's information.

A group of four men entered his room the next morning. A doctor—based on his scrubs and coat. A detective, his badge hung off his outside breast pocket on a wrinkled suit. Two lawyers accompanied them.

The detective harangued George for the better part of an hour. Over and over George said that he was injured in a sexual encounter with his girlfriend. He could remember nothing else. He asked after Liz, but the room ignored him. The doctor explained his condition, that they stabilized his arm, put a cast on it and that he might have some nerve damage. The lawyers were split. One was from the hospital. He had a ream of paperwork that needed George's signature. The doctor removed his restraints. George could see the detective make a fist and brush his sidearm. George had trouble with the pen in his left hand, but passed muster. The last lawyer was from Sherman and Sons Services. He presented George with a bill.

"Taxi fare, hotel and hospital bill for Ms. Lancaster," the lawyer said.

There was a brief pause.

"You're free to go now," the hospital's lawyer said.

"—for now," the detective said.

George was kicked out the door and into the street, a pair of scrubs along with his scraps of personal effects. Roderick hailed a cab home.

Joe waited for him on the house stoop. He drank a warm beer from a grocery bag. George sat down beside him. Joe offered a beer soon after.

"Rough night, huh?"

"Two of them, I hear," George said.

"Our friends want to show their gratitude. They want to help."

"Sherman and Sons." George ripped another beer from the bag. "That Kitty Kelly woman started all of it."

"And she's got your dead girlfriend." He sipped his beer.

"Oh my god." George dry heaved and spat flecks of foam into the bushes.

"Sorry, Ace. Whatever you kids got up to. Well. You're still vertical," Joe said. *"Let me take care of it. Pity. She had—"*

"Natural. Don't," George said.

George walked into the house to take a bath. Joe left through the back alley. As the hot water soaked across his throat, he dunked under. He held the sides of the tub with his hands and knees. He fought the burn. He controlled the desperation. George tried to will himself to stay under. Something fought back. Roderick lurched out of the water to collapse on the tile floor.

"Sad sack," Roderick said. He shaved and made himself ready in a pair of jeans and a gray t-shirt. On the stairs down from his room to the kitchen, George heard the screech of tires on the far corner down by the graveyard. George finished his tea and shuffled onto the business veranda to survey the scene. Shouts and the grinding scream of metal on metal ended with the roar of a high performance engine. George walked onto the expansive covered porch, barefoot with his empty cup in hand in time to see a man in a shiny suit, driving gloves and oversized opaque sunglasses idle by Barstow house dropping the beastly engine out of gear. The driver saluted with a loose gesture of paired fingers before laying down a layer of rubber by the driveway. The hard-top Chevelle lurched past and around the corner. Thunder from the throaty muscle car droned off, replaced by far off sirens.

"I'll do it for free," George said. "Trying to make amends. It was always business, not personal, right? So why not. You've already made sure I don't have anything else going on.

"Fine. Yes, I'll take care of the burial permits and arrangements at the cemetery. We are a rather established house.

"Very well. Bring her by when you can. The back alley has service doors for delivery, but you know that." George ended the call.

Kitty Kelly was dropped off at Barstow Funerary at eleven o'clock in the morning the next day. The driver and his passenger did not even get out to unload her body. George signed for her and wheeled the gurney into the basement. Roderick took his time with the body. She looked beautiful relaxed in repose. Most people just look dead on the table. Her extensive work was high-end. It held together except where to coroner had super glued her back together. George lit the room with candles from the showroom upstairs. Roderick turned out the lights, took a No. 10 scalpel and began to dance. Black fluid fell in splatter around the room as George cut. The blade sliced as he turned.

"*I heard you upstairs. Maniac,*" Joe said.

George stopped his spin. Coagulated fluids dripped down his arm to fall from his blade.

"*And look, we could've used that. I guess she has two ... it'll just be a little harder to market one,*" Joe said.

George turned and stared in fascination while the silicone ooze slid out through the new mouth. Surrounded by Kitty's ichor, it overcame the decomposition and pushed past like runny aspic.

"Hey, I remember this broad. Yeah, wanted new boobs like every couple months. Something about wanting to be a star. Started giving her the rejects ... yep, those are from the seventies or eighties! There, at least now we know we're not missing out too badly. I mean, they would probably have killed her if she didn't change them in the next month or so anyhow," Joe patted George on the shoulder. *"Listen, why don't you go wash up? When she due for the dirt?"*

"...three o'clock ... George said.

"Right. Rush job. I'll finish up. Sawdust is over there, where's the glue?"

George walked to a cabinet and pulled out a small caulking gun. He set it on the cabinet's shelf.

"Go wash up, get dressed. I'll see you in the kitchen. Make me a sandwich," Joe said.

Two hours later, George was dressed in a navy blue suit. A liverwurst and havarti sandwich sat on the chipped Formica table. The hearse was parked out front. George sipped a cup of sencha and leaned against the cupboard.

"Ready?" George asked.

"Just have to wash my hands," Joe said.

George turned on the water and knocked the bar of soap into the basin.

"I'll drive. Eat your sandwich," George said.

The drive to the cemetery was literally down the street.

George's ancestor founded it around a pioneer chapel made out of ancient river stone that the settlers had dug from their fields. No longer consecrated by the Church, a later ancestor purchased the land when the area incorporated. The chapel was a Barstow family trust, and they had exclusive rights to the graveyard. Used for over a hundred years, it reflected the fads of the past in faded color and crumbled stone. It was strange comfort to George. A man in a close tailored suit who never took off his driving gloves greeted their car. He stood by the open pit with his hands crossed together in front of him. His sunglasses were impenetrable crystal. Joe nodded to him as they exited the hearse. The flat lenses alternated reflections of Joe and him as George shuffled in his fugue.

"Good to see you Sergei. I see you have a new car?" Joe said.

Sergei nodded. His glasses never slipped, nor did he extend his hand or conversation. George got the impression he was there to enforce something.

"Guarding the dead against gate crashers?" George said.

Sergei remained as unyielding as Liz's nearby tombstone. They opened the back of the funeral coach and wheeled Kitty's coffin to the lowering straps. George smiled. It was the ruined coffin from the other night. The lacquer was already cracked.

"It's been an hour and a half," Joe said.

"Guess it's just us," George said.

"It was nice of Liz's family to bury her near the old chapel."

"Yeah, Sherman and Sons still cut corners. I gave them the plot for free, but they still charged the Lancasters. I let them know."

"Bastards. Charging Liz's family after they could've stopped it from happening," Joe said. *"Not like our family, eh? Well, ditch this b' and we can pay our respects to your departed over there when we're done."*

George sighed.

The gloved man patted his shoulder and left. George heard a high performance engine turn over, then the patter of gravel spit against metal.

Roderick remained for a brief moment, ostensibly to help. The crank on the lowering device slipped as Joe disappeared. Kitty came to rest with a crack of splintered wood.

Joe's laugh erupted from the broken coffin.

George screamed in madness, sinking to his knees alone.

No one heard it but *him*.

About the Author

John M. McKeel started writing while stationed in Germany with the 1st Armored Division. He wrote stories for his squad to keep up morale in the field, which led the soldiers to push him to write professionally. After duty hours and during his wife's tour of duty, John began work as a freelance features writer, travel correspondent and essayist before returning to the United States. While living in El Paso, Texas, he had his first short story "Failing St. George" published in "Tales of the Talisman" quarterly magazine, and was a food columnist for Military Spouse magazine. Upon returning to school in Virginia, Mr. McKeel was picked up by the college newspaper for his comic strip "kB" about home life with a deployed spouse. During his studies in Alexandria, he was also picked up to write a serialized collection of short stories that resulted in this novel.